PUCKER

FACTOR

MariaLisa deMora

Edited by Hot Tree Editing

First Published 2019

ISBN 13: 978-1-946738-39-4

DEDICATION

The true soldier fights not because he hates what is in front of him, but because he loves what is behind him. ~ G.K. Chesterton

To those who understand not all scars are visible.

CONTENTS

ACKNOWLEDGMENTS

The act of writing isn't courageous. Not in my eyes. Some might argue that the process of publishing is, where authors bare our souls for public entertainment. It doesn't feel courageous to me, mostly because I've gained so much from this surprising career. Being given the chance to shed light on a topic, and make it conversation-worthy—that's everything.

If you've read my other stories, you know from the very beginning veterans have often played a part. I don't always scheme to focus on them, not intentionally, not as it is within these books, where they form the true foundation for the tale. But I do love how they'll wind themselves in and amongst the heros and heroines, at times stepping forwards to take center stage, but most often providing a supporting role.

My tendency to include our military is in part because of my family. My grandfather, uncle, and of course my father all served, as did countless nephews. I remember each had a different way of dealing with difficult memories—but when the stories were told, around the bonfire, fishing on the pier, or while fixing a broken tractor axel—I was often there, listening.

My hope is they know they were heard. They were, and are, my heros.

Woofully yours,
~ML

Chapter One
Mayhan Bucklers Clubhouse

Eyes closed, Oscar Mayhan shoved his head deeper into the pillow, willing sleep to come.

It didn't. It never did on nights like this.

And it didn't matter where he was.

He could be at his home here in town, listening to the surrounding silence in his self-imposed isolation, or in this building, the clubhouse for the Mayhan Bucklers MC. A place where he was surrounded by men he was proud to call brother. Men who had walked through fire to earn the lives they lived every day. Heroes in every sense of the word, with the medals, and scars, to prove it.

At his new home, purchased only weeks ago and still unfamiliar, the sense of loneliness could become overwhelming, coloring every moment with darkness until he felt driven to be around his brothers. But while in the clubhouse, he felt small, an imposter, because his time overseas hadn't equaled what his brothers had endured.

For Oscar, there was no win.

His tours had been spent behind the wire, outwardly safe and protected by the real heroes. Of course, there had always been the threat of their enemy bringing the fight back to the bases, which did happen sometimes. When it had, Oscar had executed the drill that had been impressed on every one of them: get to the bunker, get his head down, and wait, listening to the explosions outside, way too close to where he hid along with the other men and women, assholes puckered in fear that the next whistling rocket's destination would be where they sheltered.

Assigned to the base instead of a patrol unit, he'd quickly and happily resigned himself to being a FOBBIT, someone who supported the efforts from a relatively safe location. In his case, a forward operating base, or FOB. He had every expectation he'd do his tours, earn his papers, and go home. FOBBITS weren't heroes. They were necessary cogs in the wheel that drove the military engine. FOBBITS didn't get the medals, accolades, or the girl—something he had a visceral understanding of—but of course, they also didn't often get mangled, or dead.

His VA counselor had tried to convince him that not every wound was physical, but he hadn't given the man the whole story. No one had it all. The shrink had held up

Oscar's medals as proof, but in the dank office the gleam was gone, colors faded, and he'd stared at them until it all felt as unreal as ever.

Frustrated at his thoughts, he rolled to his side, determinedly keeping his eyes closed. Maybe, unlike other nights, if he kept forcing himself to stillness, he'd sleep.

A thud down the hallway caused his eyes to fly open, and he stared into the muted darkness, listening. Moonlight leaked in around the curtains of his narrow window, and more light seeped in from underneath the single door. The thud was not repeated. There were no noises other than the normal ones that hovered over a building with more than a dozen men sleeping underneath the same roof, but the damage was done, and Oscar knew it.

"Fuck." He pushed up on that mutter, swung his legs over the edge of the bed, and sat slumped for a moment, trying to talk himself out of what he was about to do. With another muttered, "Fuck it," he reached for his phone.

Sleep was elusive on the best of nights, and when he gave in to the urges to tear his slowly healing wounds wide, it would be a stranger.

Using the app on his phone, Oscar navigated to his online storage, then through a maze of folders until he found the one he wanted. Generically named, so if someone did stumble on it, they'd never know how important it was. He clicked on the icon and waited with held breath, as he always did. There was an absurd fear that somehow, someway, the pictures would be gone.

They never were.

Oscar slid his fingertip over the image on the screen, moving to the next, and the next. Pictures of him, and her. Smiling faces that gradually lost their glow, expressions darkening until in the final few both were almost scowling. The very last image was different; the woman was back to happy but with a different actor in frame. Professionally shot, the picture focused on a bride all in white, her groom in dress uniform, her bent backwards over his arm—and even through the kiss, Oscar could see her smile.

She'd wanted a hero, and she got one.

It just wasn't him.

Chapter Two
Lindsay

Fingers white-knuckling the unpadded plastic arms of the wheelchair she'd been made to sit in, Lindsay Ashworth tried to breathe through the tightening around her belly, a pain that morphed and darted straight to her back, blooming into an overwhelming agony. She endured this quietly, eyes closed, consciously relaxing her arms and shoulders until her hands rested easily on her lap. She let the rest of the contraction roll over and through her, and once it had eased, she blinked and looked again to the man filling out her registration paperwork.

"Sorry," she told him, hating how there were quiet fractures through that single word.

"Don't be, Ms. Ashworth. You do what you need to do, and we'll get through this and get you up to the OB folks fast as we can." She glanced at the nameplate on the desk, frowning when it didn't give her his name, declaring instead that this area belonged to a feminine-sounding Leticia Moses. He noticed the direction of her gaze and grinned, then chuckled as he said, "Nope, not me. I'm Oscar, Oscar Mayhan, and I'm filling in for Ticia for a little bit."

"Pleased to meet you…" Lindsay's voice trailed off as her fingers tightened around each other, hidden from his view by the edge of the desk. She blinked slowly, taking in a deep breath to try and stave off the unexpected beginnings of the next contraction, and finished, "Mr. Mayhan."

"Are you havin' another one? Already?"

She nodded. His reference to the rapid onset of yet another exhausting contraction ratcheted up the anxiety already causing her heart to trip along in double-time. After hours spent on her own, battling through the fear that it was happening, really happening—her pregnancy was coming to its inevitable conclusion, and here she was, alone—she'd hoped the staff at the small, country hospital would give her more confidence. Oscar Mayhan was nice, seemed compassionate, and could clearly read a situation, but she wanted someone who would take charge.

"I'm thinkin' we need to go on and hustle you upstairs now, Ms. Ashworth, before your water breaks."

Forcing a smile, she shook her head and began to count, hitting ninety before she'd finished breathing through the pain. She pulled in a quick breath once it eased, the forced tension leaving her muscles aching. "Too late, that was about three blocks before I got here."

He stared at her. Then his gaze swung to look out the windows of the tiny office they were in, door closed for her privacy. She didn't know what he'd see but knew what he wouldn't find in the waiting area, because she hadn't brought anyone with her. *Hard to do that when I don't know anyone in town.* "Who's out there for you?"

Lindsay stared at him silently, willing him to drop a topic he couldn't know still hurt so much.

"Ma'am, you need an emergency contact, at least."

Clearing her throat of the painful knot that developed instantly, she shook her head again. "No contacts." The expression on his face was confused, a puzzlement that didn't clear at her words.

"Nobody with you?"

She stared at him, hating the way his face softened. *God, he's persistent.* She'd bet he got his way on a lot of things just in this fashion, wearing someone down with repeated restatements of the original question. In this case, there would be no other answer.

He tried a final time. "Nobody?"

Lindsay kept her eyes on him and saw when his steady gaze focused on the trembling of her lips. She watched him wrestle with something for a moment, saw the instant he made a decision, and stared as he rolled his chair back and stood up. He opened a door at the back of the room and yelled out, "Molly, I'm takin' off."

What?

"What?" A woman's voice responded immediately, echoing Lindsay's internal reaction, but instead of terror the woman's irritation was clear. "You said you'd work while I at least ate lunch, Oscar. Ticia left me in the lurch, man. Help a sister out."

"One, you're not my sister, and you aren't the ole lady of any of my brothers." He grabbed a jacket from the coat tree beside the door Lindsay had come through. "So you're not a sister, honey. You're a lifelong friend, and I love you like a sister, but that's not something you can claim on your own. I'm takin' off, but there's nobody waiting. You're good."

Lindsay stared at him, that knot back in residence deep in her throat, tears threatening to spill over as the clamping pain around her middle struck true and hard, banded again through the hot coal it woke in the middle of her back. *Nobody waiting*. He was right; she was nobody to him. Less than nobody, she was an irritation, with no good answers to his questions. She bowed her head and waited for him to leave, breathing in and out through her nose slowly. Hands cradling her stomach, she stroked the hardened uterine walls covered by soft skin, jolting when the baby inside her stretched and pushed, clearly not enjoying the cramped quarters.

She startled again when the chair she was in moved, backing out through the now-open door. She looked up in time to see a pretty girl stick her head into the office, her mouth an *O* of surprise.

"What?" That was all Lindsay could get out around the pain as the chair turned and took off at an alarming speed past the entry doors and towards what looked like a bank of elevators.

Craning her neck, she looked up and found Oscar Mayhan striding along behind the chair, hands on the grips to steer it. He slapped the call button for the elevators and, when one opened immediately, backed the chair in like he'd done it a thousand times before.

"Oh." Lindsay dipped her head as her eyes closed when the wave of pain hit full force. Focusing on her breathing, she scarcely noticed the bump as the wheelchair left the elevator and only vaguely was aware of Mr. Mayhan speaking to someone. Then they were moving up another hallway. Heat enveloped her hands, and without thinking, she twisted in the grip and clutched back tightly, breathing faster than she wanted, panting as the pain spiraled up and out of control.

"You're doin' great, Ms. Ashworth." A woman's comforting voice came from just behind her, then asked, "Oscar, how frequent are they?"

"Had her in the office for only a handful of minutes, between that and the elevator, and this one, probably half a dozen in twenty minutes, max." Something touched her face and she leaned away, stopping her attempted evasion when it chased her, settling on her cheek and jaw. "She's hot, Debby. Burnin' up. Said her water broke 'three blocks ago,' and those are her exact words to me. I'm guessing she walked in like this."

"Where's her family, the baby's father?" The woman's voice was sharper, something Lindsay noted because the contraction was easing, waning as rapidly as it had come on. She thought for a moment that sharp tone was directed at her, but the fear bubbling inside her was put to rest as the woman, Debby, said, "Something as precious as a baby comin' to air, and there's no one to celebrate with her. Their loss, Oscar. We'll get her through."

Lindsay lifted her head and had to blink, because Mr. Mayhan was crouched in front of her, one hand wrapped around hers, one reached up to her face. "You doin' okay, Ms. Ashworth?" His low, gravel-filled voice was rough but gentle at the same time, and that beauty went hand in hand with the handsome that was all of him. Dark hair, mostly dark beard, small strands of silver worked in high on his sideburns, and the most gorgeous green eyes currently turned to her with grave intensity. "It's backed off?" She nodded. "Then up you get. We'll settle you in a bed."

Debby, someone Lindsay suspected was an OB nurse, said, "I'll get an orderly."

"I got it." Mr. Mayhan flipped the brake levers on the chair. Then his hand wrapped around Lindsay's ankle and gently lifted her foot off the rest and onto the floor, then repeated the process with her other foot.

"Oscar, I need to get her into a gown."

He froze in place, half raised from his crouch, and looked over Lindsay's head for a long minute, then clipped out one word, "Right." Gaze back to Lindsay's face, he stared at her for a moment before he said in that low, rumbling voice, "You can trust me." Lindsay licked her lips, not understanding the darkness that moved over his expression as his gaze dropped, then lifted again. "Lindsay, right?" She found herself unexpectedly shy, tucking her chin to her throat in a truncated nod. "I'm Oscar."

Forcing out the words, she acknowledged his reintroduction. "Yeah. Mr. Mayhan. You said."

He shook his head firmly. "I'm Oscar."

"Oscar," she parroted, and he smiled, lips curling up as his eyes narrowed, sun lines trailing off from the corners, tattling about the amount of time he spent outside. The easy way his mouth curved into the expression told her smiling was something else he did a lot, too. He was good at taking charge, too, and she had a moment to appreciate whatever had helped make him this way.

"Debby's gonna need some help getting you into a hospital gown." Lindsay sucked in a breath, suddenly understanding. Undressed, she'd be vulnerable, naked in more ways than he knew, because for months now she'd been the only witness to the changes in her body. "I can go get that help, or I can be that help. Way things are going, movin' along at a pretty quick pace here, I'm thinking we need to get you into that bed sooner rather than later."

A woman stepped into view, and from her thinned lips and tilted head, Lindsay read she wasn't as on-board with this idea as Oscar was. "I need to get vitals, and a history."

"And she needs to be where she can get comfortable, so you can take care of her like she needs," Oscar shot back, never taking his gaze off Lindsay's face. "Lindsay Ashworth, twenty-nine, new resident of Mayhan. Full-term pregnancy, active labor. There, that's your history." It seemed Oscar had been listening to her disjointed responses to his earlier questions. "Lindsay, we'll do this fast and private. Then you'll be comfortable. Get the door, Deb."

Debby disappeared for a moment, then was back in front of Lindsay with a bundle of fabric in her hands, the door clunking into the frame behind her.

"Let's get ready, Lindsay." Oscar took the material and shook it out, and Lindsay saw it was a gown printed with tiny pacifiers and bottles, diaper pins and strollers.

"First change her top. Then we'll stand her and get the bottoms off."

Eyes on Lindsay's face, Oscar nodded at Debby's words, then Lindsay saw only the top of his head for the moments it took him to remove her shoes and socks. Lindsay watched as he set them aside, socks tucked inside just like she would have done.

He leaned into her and captured her with his gaze again. "Eyes on me, okay?" Lindsay stared at him and he held her gaze, waiting for her nod. Then her jacket was gone, followed by her sweater, and her bra was unhooked and drooping on her arms. Oscar deftly removed it, then leaned even closer as he slipped the gown up her arms. A quick movement behind her head and he shifted back, gripping her forearms as he urged her with a soft, "Up, honey." Ignoring the returning tightness around her middle, she grabbed hold and stood, pushing through the growing pain to stand upright. "Get her pants, Deb."

The chair moved; then there were deft fingers at her waist, her pants and panties whisked down her legs, hands urging her to lift first one foot, then the other.

"Got one comin' on?" Oscar hadn't looked away from her face, and he had a pair of lines between his brows, something that told her he worried just as much as he smiled. She nodded, back bowing as the contraction pulled all of her muscles painfully tight. "Hold on to me, Lindsay. I got you." He released one of her arms and towed her closer to him so she could lean against his strong frame. "I got you." She clutched at his shirt, head turned into him, so her face was hidden when the pain pulled a groan out of her.

"You weren't kidding. I'm glad you got her up here when you did." Something cold and slippery touched the inside of Lindsay's thighs and she jolted, head coming upright. "Lindsay, I'm just going to check where this little one's at, see how eager they are to join the party." Probing touches, then Debby hissed, "Goodness, you're right there, aren't you?" Her voice gentled as she reported, "Good news, Lindsay. You're definitely in labor.

13

Plus four station, which means your baby's dropped into the birth canal, and I'm going to say eight centimeters dilated. Where do you feel the pain, Lindsay, can you show me, honey?"

"My back," Lindsay mangled the words, groaning again as the contraction peaked finally, leaving her shaking in the pain's slowly ebbing wake. "When it's strong like that, it's my back mostly."

"Posterior presentation," came the unfathomable response. "Oscar, I'll go get a squat bar, if you can hold her like that for a minute? We'll do what we can to make it better. She's not too far for an epi, but that'll mean she's bed-bound for the duration."

"I don't want an epidural," Lindsay said, shaking her head, which had the effect of grinding her forehead against Oscar's chest. "I can do this."

"We know you can, Lindsay." Oscar's beautiful, gruff voice came from just over her head, the rumbling words vibrating through his chest and into her. "Women have been doing this for centuries, but that don't mean you can't be as comfortable as we can make it for you. That baby inside you is facin' the wrong way for an easy birth, so what Deb's talking about is using some positioning to convince that little one to flip around."

"What? No, I've been feeling feet stretching high up." The sudden panic flooding through her forced out the question she'd most feared asking, "The baby, my baby's okay, right?" Terror drove the movement as she lifted her head and looked at him, the feeling easing as she watched that softness settled on his features again.

"Yeah, right as rain," Debby said over the snap and pop of a glove being removed. "And not breech, this little one is head down, no worries there. But they've got the rear part of their head pressing against your back, which is why it's hurting more than it should. Do you know the sex of the baby?" Lindsay shook her head, not meeting Debby's eyes as she anticipated the next question. "Who's your OB? I'll call them in when I pass by the desk." Eyes closed, Lindsay dipped her chin to her throat and shook her head again. "Oscar said you haven't been in Mayhan long? What about your hometown OB, did you get your records from them?" Lindsay didn't answer, keeping her face angled away. "Tell you what, honey"— Deb's voice softened—"we'll get you settled and I'll call my favorite doc, give him an update and get him in here. How does that sound?"

"Sounds." Lindsay broke off to clear her throat. "Sounds good." She twisted and shoved out a lungful of air. "Oh." Oscar's arm tightened around her shoulders. "Mmm." He moved, and she went with him, shuffling around to the end of the bed, breathing shallowly as another powerful contraction began its process of sweeping over her. When he tried to take her hand from his chest, she tightened her fingers in his shirt, holding on, irrationally afraid he was about to leave her here alone.

"Gonna get you some relief, Lindsay. Trust me." His voice was already so familiar that she panted softly and turned loose. He wrapped her fingers around the footboard, then stepped to her side and placed her other hand there, too. His arm slipped under her arm and around her chest, his other going to her lower back. "Come down here with me. Come on." Feet spread as wide as she could, she tried to do what he asked, but it felt as if she was going to topple over, even with him holding her from the side like he was. "I got you, Lindsay. Feet flat on the floor, squat down between my legs."

She slowly lowered herself, and the moment she was in position, his hand left her back, coming to the side of her head, where he gently pushed sideways until her cheek rested on his chest. Once she'd relaxed into him as much as she could, the heat from his touch returned to her back, where his fingers started rubbing hard, digging deep into the tight muscles at the top of her butt. That pressure felt so incredibly good she sagged against him with a sigh and a groan. Immediately the contraction felt more manageable, less overwhelming, and when she said, "Oh," this time, it was in relief. It felt good to have her arms stretched up, and the tightening around her belly seemed more purposeful than just pain. With Oscar's thumb and fingers stroking the muscles rhythmically and firmly, the crushing pain in her back was muted enough she could breathe through the contraction.

"Yeah, that's the ticket." He shifted, the knee in front of her legs going down to the floor. "We got this, Lindsay. We got this."

She didn't know when it had gone from being her chore to their shared goal, but she'd take it. The trek to the hospital had her strangled with dread when her water broke, leaving her holding on to a street sign as a puddle of liquid grew around her feet. After feeling alone and afraid for so long—when the veil of fear pulled back, just as the pain had, it gave her a moment to breathe and she accepted it like the blessing it was.

"Mmm." Eyes closed tightly, she waited it out, the final tension from the contraction falling away. "That's so much better."

"You steady like that? Got a good hold?" Lindsay lifted her head and angled her eyes up, seeing Oscar smiling down at her. She nodded. "Okay, stay just like that." He slowly released his grip on her far side, fingers relaxing and retreating. Lindsay shivered as she lost the heat from his arm. He stayed close for another moment, then reassured her, "You're good." A moment later, he was behind her, and she saw his knees on the floor between her legs. Belatedly she realized the gown gaped at the back, because how else would he have been rubbing her bare skin. Then she lost that thought when his hands gripped low on each hip, thumbs firmly drilling directly into where it had hurt so badly. "Get this loosened up, and the next one won't be as bad." From his mutter, she suspected he was looking down, and Lindsay tried to ignore the knowledge that her bare butt would be on full display. "How's that, Lindsay?"

"Really good." She rolled her head, trying to wipe the side of her face. "Are you a nurse or something?"

17

"Or something. I'm a little bit of everything these days."

His answer didn't make any sense, but she set that aside, breathing slowly

He asked, "What kind of work do you do?"

"I was a marketer." Neck bending forwards and back, she stretched out her shoulders, hoping he'd leave it at that.

He let her breathe through a few more contractions, his voice soothing and encouraging, just his presence making it so she wasn't as afraid. It helped to know that for now, in this moment, she was no longer alone. Finally, he asked the question she'd hoped he wouldn't.

"*Was* a marketer? Where'd you work?"

She named the Dallas firm she'd worked at for five years, moving between the different offices as clients and projects demanded. It had been her dream job until seven months ago, when she'd told her lover she was pregnant. Lindsay left out that detail, as well as the information that her boss was the baby's sperm donor. He'd made it clear he didn't want to be a dad, writing her a check to "take care of the little problem," and when she hadn't, he'd conspired with the head HR director—his wife, something Lindsay hadn't known given the woman had a different last name, worked at the home office, and neither of them wore rings—to get her out of the firm quickly and quietly.

"How'd you get to Mayhan? It's a fair distance to D-Town."

She pulled in a breath to answer him, then blew it out steadily as another contraction hit. "Mmm." It was strong, maybe the strongest yet, but in this position, they were no longer threatening to tear her apart like the previous ones had. "Mmm." The heat from his hands grounded her, his voice soothing her through that contraction and into the next. They were coming in waves now, relentlessly moving things forwards, each growing in frequency and urgency.

Through it all, he told her with words and deeds, "I got you, Lindsay. You can do this." Oscar repeated it until she believed him, and even though her legs were shaking from the strain, she felt strong and capable.

The band around her belly tightened, and tightened again until something shifted inside her. With the change, that band of tightness clamped down hard until she couldn't push out any more air, her body bearing down. Now her arms were shaking, palms slick with sweat threatening to slip on the metal of the footboard as she tried to renew her grip.

"Hold on." Oscar's heat disappeared for a moment, and she heard something dragging across the floor, then he was behind her again, lifting under her arms until she was positioned between his knees. "Get your elbows on my legs. See if you can hold yourself up like this."

Feet still flat on the floor, this was more a suspended sitting position, and she looked down to see the shape of her stomach had changed, no longer a hard beachball riding high. "Oscar." She let her head drop back and looked up at him. "Something's going on."

His hands swept up and down her arms, massaging her shoulders and neck before his fingers hit her temples, rubbing slow circles. "Yeah, things are progressing." She stared at his corded neck, visible behind that beard she liked a lot, and she wanted to put her mouth on him. Heat swept over her at the bizarrely timed thought, and she averted her face, looking back at her belly. He asked, "How's your back now?"

With shock, she realized it didn't hurt, not like it had. "It's good." She shoved her elbows against his thighs, testing how it felt to push up. "It's really good."

"Bet when Deb checks you again, that stubborn little fella's gonna be in a better place to make his entrance." Through her movements, he'd kept his grip on the side of her face, fingertips drawing tiny circles on each temple. "Just needed to let Mother Nature do her work."

"He?" She smiled, surprised at how bubbly she felt. "Are you taking bets?"

"Oh, yeah. Do you know any girl as tenacious as that?" He chuckled, the sound a dark musical tone that filled the room. "I don't. Nope, this is a boy. No doubt."

"How do you know all this?" She adjusted herself slightly, resting her back against him. "Do you have kids?"

He was quiet, too quiet, and she was afraid she'd asked something she shouldn't. The muscles under her arms tightened, bunched, and shifted while the silence piled up, building a mountain of deadened air she felt was suffocating her. "No, Lindsay. No kids." The pain in his voice was real and jagged, baggage that would wear him down. She knew, having carried that same kind of weight for so long. "I just know a little about a lot, and this is one of those. My sister's first child was the same, and her husband talked a dozen times about the miracle worker nurse who fixed it by getting Patty out of bed. Figured it was worth a try."

Another contraction hit, and she closed her mouth, breathing in and out through her nose, slowly. "Mmm." Without the horrendous back pain, she could stay ahead of it even as it swelled, going with the pain as it went past cramping that would have doubled her over, rising until every muscle was strung tight before it ebbed. She groaned again, unable to keep the sounds quiet. "Mmm." The contraction backed off much slower this time, her uterus staying rigid under her skin as she trailed her fingertips back and forth across it, distracting herself from the pain.

There was noise in the hallway beyond the door, and then Debby was there, hands full of all kinds of things. "Doc's on his way. I've got ice chips and an ice bag. The squat bar isn't anywhere to be found, which probably means maintenance tucked it behind something in some closet. I've got a call in to Dale to ask about it, but who knows when he'll come out of the woods today." Her steps paused a beat as she took them in, but then she was back to business. "Good move, Oscar. You're a champ. Lindsay, I need to ask a few questions but nothing too tough. You don't have to move. I'll come to you for what I need."

Once everything was arranged on a rolling table, Debby dragged it across the room and squatted down next to Lindsay. The nurse wrapped a blood pressure cuff around her upper arm, left it dangling as she held a device to Lindsay's forehead, humming when it beeped. Then she pressed firmly on her feet and watched for a moment, mouth moving silently, did something at her ankles, made the same silent counting thing before she whipped her stethoscope from around her neck, and pumped the bulb on the blood pressure cuff to take a reading.

Through all of it, Oscar's fingers never stopped moving. He'd gone from her temples down to the back and sides of her neck, then across her shoulders and over the upper curves of her arms. Everywhere he touched, he left behind a relaxed lethargy that Lindsay knew wouldn't last.

"Lindsay, do you know when you're due?"

"A week. My dad's birthday." No matter the circumstances surrounding this pregnancy, he would have loved a grandchild.

"You want me to call him?" Debby's question was gently probing, and Lindsay shook her head slowly.

"He's been gone not quite two years now." She closed her eyes. "There's nobody, sorry."

"Nothing you have to be sorry about." Oscar's gruff voice soothed her. "And you're not alone. Not today. I got you, Lindsay."

Debby's voice had resumed her down-to-business tone, something Lindsay realized helped make the questions less personal. "How long have you been in labor?"

Lindsay considered, then tallied up the hours before sharing. "Yesterday morning. When I woke up, it felt like a mule kicked me in the back."

"Yesterday morning?" Oscar's voice was disbelieving, and she glanced up to see his jaw had grown tight.

"Yeah. The morning news was on the radio. I'd read it takes a long time for first-time moms, so I stayed there until the pain got so bad." After a while even reclining on the hotel bed hadn't been restful, so Lindsay had found herself pacing circles around the tiny suite of rooms. She turned her gaze back to Debby, searching for answers in her expression. "Did I do wrong? Did I hurt my baby?"

"No, honey. You did right. Labor's always easier in familiar surroundings, so it's good you were at home." *Home*, Lindsay silently echoed the incorrect word with an agonizing sadness before forcing herself to listen to Debby's next question. "Did you have any care, honey?"

"I went to a clinic for a few months. I take my vitamins, and they did all the tests and stuff. But I had to leave Dallas, and I've...kind of skipped around." That was an understatement, because she'd been following cash-paying freelance and temporary jobs, living in extended stay hotels until she had to find another position and move again. "Mayhan, the city here hired me to do a campaign for them. I'm supposed to have my first meeting tomorrow."

"That'll have to wait." Debby wasn't looking at her, so she didn't see how her words hit hard. Without that job, Lindsay couldn't afford to stay anywhere, and her meager savings wouldn't keep a child in diapers for long. "I'm going to check you again." She turned back with a glove on one hand, fingers shining with whatever she'd doused them with. "Hold still, Lindsay."

Just as she said that, the biggest contraction so far hit Lindsay hard, and she bowed forwards with the force, her elbows nearly skidding off Oscar's legs. He caught her, hands under her arms as he hauled her back against his chest.

"Oscar," Debby said, holding her hand up, gaze fixed between Lindsay's legs. "We need her in that bed." A pause, and Lindsay quit listening because her body was demanding she do something. Something specific. She tightened her hands around Oscar's knees and hunched over more, chin to her chest. "Now, Oscar. She's gonna have that baby."

The room shifted and swung around, and she lost her grip as Oscar moved. Arms under her knees and behind her back, he lifted her against his chest and a moment later was gently depositing her on the bed. Her hands immediately went to the rails he and Debby raised at the sides of the bed, and Lindsay planted her feet before pulling hard, straining. "Ohh."

"Doc gonna make it?" Oscar's question should have frightened Lindsay, but she was focused on what was changing inside her. The intentional demands of her body were shaping into something. The straining lasted another few seconds before she fell backwards, panting. Debby must have answered him, because his clipped, "Okay. Tell me what to do," caught her off guard. Staring up at him, she felt another swell of whatever was happening move through her. "Deb, help me out here."

"She's in a good position. Just support her back on the next contraction. Lindsay, you're going to push for me, okay? Your baby's in a hurry, and that's not a bad thing, but we've got to ease through parts of this, so stop pushing when I tell you to, okay?" Lindsay stared at her for a second, not comprehending. "We're going again, you ready?"

"Ready," Oscar said, shoving his arm behind her and lifting. Lindsay reached for the rails, gripping firmly before she tucked her chin to her chest and pushed. And pushed. And pushed, holding her breath. Something changed inside her body again, a lessening of that pressure, a different relief than before, and Oscar was in her face, telling her firmly, "Lindsay, stop now. Stop pushing."

She shook her head, staring at him. What he'd asked was impossible. "I have to. Please. I have to." Huge breath in, and tuck, and push, push, push, then a surprised breath because it was over. There was a slithering release from inside her, and a moment later, she saw her baby lying on the mattress between her feet. Wiggling and squirming, it was coated all over in something white, dark hair matted with liquid and blood, but there was a silence so profound she felt it pressing in against her. "Please."

"You've got a boy. Oscar, he's got an Apgar of seven." Debby's voice was light and joyous as she scooped the baby up, careful of the trailing cord, and wrapped him in a blanket before she leaned close, holding him out to Lindsay.

Reverently, she took him in her arms, cradling him to her chest as his mouth opened and he took in a big breath, then with a shaking chin, cried out for the first time. "Oh my God." His trembling wail struck arrow-straight into her heart and Lindsay started crying. "Oh my God."

Oscar chuckled when he said, "Correction, he's a nine."

His words didn't make any sense, so Lindsay corrected his correction, stating what she firmly believed. "No, he's a ten. Definitely a ten." She gazed into her son's face, that first cry having led to a second and a third before trailing off. "Hey, you," she cooed as he stared up at her. "Look at you. Just look at you." She eased the blanket back to count his fingers, then his toes, and cradled his head with her hand. "Look at you."

Oscar's voice was gruff when he said, "He's gorgeous, Lindsay."

There was a tug behind her head, then the gown slipped down until it barely covered her breasts. Instinctively, she shifted her son and laid him against her skin, keeping her gaze on his tiny face.

"He is, isn't he? Look at you, baby boy. Just look at you."

A hand appeared, then drifted backwards, and without looking up, she reached out and took hold of Oscar, bringing his hand close until the backs of his curled knuckles brushed her son's cheek. "He's perfect."

"He is." She looked up at Oscar, seeing a wonder on his face she knew was reflected on her own. "Oscar Mayhan, meet Christopher Sage Ashworth." She cuddled her newborn son closer. "Thank you." Throat tight, she struggled but finally got out the rest of what she wanted to say. "What you did for me. For us. Everything. Thank you."

Chapter Three
Oscar

He stood against the wall beside the door, eyes on Lindsay and Christopher. Debby had finally had a chance to grab another nurse to come in and help Lindsay deliver the placenta while Debby took the baby to the nursery to do the needed measurements. Proud as any aunt, she'd announced to him as she whisked past with Christopher in her arms, "Seven pounds, fourteen ounces, twenty-two inches long. He's a big boy, Oscar."

Doc Cullman had come in after that, chatted with Deb while he reviewed Lindsay's chart even as he covertly watched how the woman was with her child, then sat on the edge of the bed and talked to her, looking every inch the doting grandfather he was. He'd put her at ease in moments, until she'd willingly given her son up to him to look over. Then, when he'd finished with the baby, he'd glanced at Oscar with a strange look in his eye, marched to where he stood, and deposited Christopher in his arms.

Oscar's heart pounded with the remembered terror. He'd frozen in place, afraid he would drop the child. He'd stared down into that tiny face, filled with big eyes and topped with a dark head of hair peeking out from under his knitted cap, and immediately fallen in love. Christopher had studied him for a moment, then yawned, and with a tiny mew like a kitten, turned his head until he found the side of his fist. He sucked for a while, his efforts slowing gradually until Oscar realized the infant had drifted to sleep in his arms, and he fell just a little harder.

Deb's appropriation of the baby had been unwelcome, but he'd glimpsed Lindsay's eager face over Deb's shoulder and did his best to remind himself of his part in all this. Support when needed, and now, he was no longer necessary.

Story of my life.

"Did you hear me?" Deb was looking at him, and he shook his head. "Oscar Mayhan, it's nearly nine o'clock. You've been here for hours, and labor and delivery is exhausting work. You're dead on your feet. You should head home."

He looked past her to see Lindsay had Christopher held to her breast, face flushed and smiling. She stroked the boy's head as he nursed, tugging down the tiny cap that covered that mop of hair. "She need anything?" He kept his voice quiet, not wanting to disturb the new mother and baby. "Anything at all, Deb?"

"Not right now. I'll get her set up best I can, but she'll only be here a couple of days. She's going to need a lot of help when she gets discharged."

He watched Lindsay's mouth curve up into a smile as Christopher's hand curled around her finger, holding on. As if she felt the weight of his gaze on her, she looked up and turned that brilliant, soft smile in his direction, and Oscar felt it in his gut like a velvet blow.

"I got her, Deb. You keep me updated, but I'm down for anything she needs." Deb narrowed her eyes but finally nodded. "Lindsay," he called softly and waited for her to look back at him, her attention already absorbed by her child again. *As it should be.* "I'll come see you tomorrow, yeah?" With a come-here gesture, she held her hand out, and he eased closer until he could take it in his. She tugged, pulling him until he was staring down at tiny Christopher happily latched onto his momma's breast, jaw and cheek working as he nursed. Oscar couldn't help it; he stroked along the softest baby's skin he'd ever touched, gliding his fingertip across Christopher's cheek to his ear until he could cradle the boy's head. "I'll see you tomorrow, too, little boy."

"Oscar." He glanced up at Lindsay's face, struck again by her beauty. Even exhausted, something shown by the lines in her face, she was gorgeous. "You'll be back, right?"

"Yeah, Lindsay. I'll be back." He lifted his hand and brushed a kiss across his fingertips, then pressed that to Christopher's temple, gentle and soft. "Wouldn't miss it."

Walking back to the clubhouse through the darkness, he ran the day back through his head, the feeling of wonder never leaving him. He'd watched her come through the entryway doors, hand pressed tight against the side of her belly, and had been up and out of his borrowed chair in an instant. She hadn't argued the wheelchair, thank goodness, but he cursed himself again that he hadn't realized her black pants were wet, water already broken on her lonely trek to the hospital.

He'd kept waiting for someone to walk in and claim her. Expected they'd dropped her off at the doors to park a vehicle and would rush in to be with her. Lindsay's lack of awareness of the doors opening and closing should have been his first clue that she was alone. She'd told him she thought she was in labor but hadn't seemed distressed, and it had been several minutes before he realized she was experiencing contractions right there in the office, burying whatever she was feeling in a calm façade and quiet words.

With Debby being Doc Cullman's niece, he trusted her to do the right thing, but Oscar hadn't been able to leave Lindsay to her care. *I just wanted to help.* He suppressed the truth that he hadn't been capable of forcing himself away.

Through it all, Lindsay held to her soft words, gentle nature, not turning into the kind of harridan TV dramas made a man expect to see in that situation. And Oscar had felt honored to help in whatever small way he could. Keeping her calm, rubbing the tension away, even supporting her at the end—she'd been determined, and all he could do was ride alongside her all the way.

Her beauty, which had been considerable, had compounded and grown as she held her baby. Cradling little Christopher close, she'd looked the epitome of motherhood. Proud and protective, caring and nurturing, Lindsay was all of that and more.

Crazy days.

He nearly tripped on a curb and looked up to see he'd walked the full eight blocks without noticing. Another twenty strides farther, and he turned to climb the steps leading into the clubhouse, a building that had been his grandfather's home at one time. Taking the steps two at a time, he made it to the porch and yanked open the door, looking around to see who was in attendance. His cousin Kirby Westbrook and two members, Donny Doss and Walt Peters, were standing in the kitchen area, leaning on three sides of the island, beers in hand.

"Hey," he called, walking towards them.

Kirby straightened and gave him a puzzled look, repeating his greeting, "Hey." He tipped his head to the side. "I thought you were only supposed to be at the hospital for lunch?"

"Way past noon, Oscar." Donny grinned at him.

"Yeah, had a—" He stopped, unsure how to characterize today in a way that would convey the wonder he still felt. *A miracle.*

"Had a what?" Kirby set his beer down and stared at Oscar, concern darkening his expression. "You okay, brother?"

That summed up the club. Mayhan Bucklers MC had been his and Kirby's grandfather's motorcycle club, forged after the man's service to his country ended, then fallen to ruin following his death. Kirby had come back from his overseas duty changed, his TBI a challenge set to make his life hard, but he'd had the idea to resurrect the club in a different way. They were a group of combat-injured veterans—except for Oscar—who'd banded together to lift up and support each other. Kirby's vision made flesh and carried out by example every day.

"Yeah, brother. I'm good. Just had the most amazing thing happen today." Oscar took the beer Walt held out, popped the top, and drank deep. "Amazing."

"Do tell? Share, my man. I could use a little amazing today." Donny stretched, then jerked his thumb over his shoulder at the media room, where Oscar could hear the muted sounds of video games. "Brain's in there makin' life a misery for everyone."

"What's up with Brian?" Brian Nelson, also called Brain, had been in the MBMC for as long as any of the men Oscar and Kirby had recruited, and like many of them, he still struggled with the demons left from his time in the military. His TBI symptoms were relentless and plagued every aspect of his life with anger, flashes of forgotten memories, and despair. "You have to call the doc?" He looked at Kirby, who was shaking his head. "What's he need, brother?"

"Just someone to sit with him, mostly. We've been trading off back and forth today." There was a loud burst of gunfire from the video game, the sound real enough Oscar had to curb his instinct to duck, and he saw the other men doing the same. "Sounds like he needs another body to be in his space." More than any of them, Brian found it easy to get lost in the controlled violence of his favorite first-person shooter games, and having someone to balance reality with the world on the screen helped anchor him.

"Tell us your news, first." Walt tipped the top of his beer towards Oscar. "I wanna hear about some amazing, too."

"Woman walked into admitting. I was filling in for Ticia since she's out with her little girl sick." All three men nodded. Leticia was known and a favorite, showing up at the clubhouse on weekends when she had a sitter, and hanging out to watch movies and drink a beer or two. She'd hooked up with a couple of the men, after making it clear that was all she wanted, so she didn't cause problems between brothers. "So this woman walked in by herself, already in labor. I took her upstairs, and Deb was pretty much on her own there in OB, so I stuck around. I've never...she was a trouper, didn't really complain about anything, just tried to get through it best she could." He took a drink, surprised to see every eye turned towards him, the men avidly listening. "It took a little bit, couple of hours, but she had a little boy."

"Jesus. You delivered her baby?" Kirby shook his head. "That's something else, Oscar."

"No, Deb did that part, I just was there for Lindsay." He wrapped both hands around the can and rested it on the island. His heart pounded at the memory. He cleared his throat and told them a truth he'd found out today, "It's a profound thing, to be there when a life's beginning."

"Amen, brother. That's a thing to be proud of. No matter your role, just being present is humbling." Walt lifted his beer in a salute. "To our brother, the baby whisperer."

"Fuck you." Oscar laughed when the men raised their cans and echoed Walt's words. "She's a good little momma. She reached out and latched onto that boy, and the look on her face was...like he was the most important thing in her life. Devotion like I've never seen, right there in front of me." He remembered Deb's reflected pride in Lindsay, how she'd put voice to what had been in his head when she declared they'd get Lindsay through it all. *She's got nobody here, though. Doesn't even know anyone except me and Deb.* Single mom, not just on her own, but doing that in a town where she was a stranger. He drew his brows down, scowling as he told them, "She's in a tough spot, though. She came to town to work, but she'll be laid up for a while."

"Her people can help her, right?" Kirby was staring at him with a strange expression, frowning when Oscar shook his head. "She's got people, right? Has someone comin' for her?"

Trust him to drill straight to the piece that bugs me the most. "No, man. She walked in alone, said she's got nobody in town. She's from the Dallas area, but it didn't sound like she'd been there in a while." He sighed, remembering the sadness in Lindsay's voice when she told him there was no one in the waiting room for her. "Deb's going to see what kind of info she can get and let me know. I'll help if I can."

"What's she do?" Kirby took a step back, resting a hip against the countertop, one arm crossed over his chest. This was his thinking mode, and Oscar grinned to see him tackling a problem that would never impact him, just because it was the right thing to do. "For work, I mean."

"She's a marketer, said the city hired her for something. I'm betting she's either at the BnB here in town or that rent-by-the-week motel out near the highway." He mentally measured the distance she would have walked to the hospital from either and winced. "I'll call the Chamber of Commerce tomorrow, see what they say."

"If she's looking for work, we could use some help with a few things I want to do with the foundation." Kirby shrugged. "It's an option."

"One worth exploring." Oscar nodded. "I'll keep it in mind." He thought again about how Lindsay looked in the bed, her small newborn cradled to her chest. "It would be flexible hours and stuff—that'll be important now that she's got little Christopher."

"Christopher?" Walt retrieved another beer from the refrigerator. "That her boy?"

"Christopher Sage. She didn't hesitate to name him, seemed to be about the only thing she'd thought through with him." Exhaustion in the form of a yawn hit him suddenly, jaw-crackingly huge, and he shook his head when it passed finally. "Jesus, I'm tired. If I go in and sit with Brian, I'll be asleep in five minutes. If one of you can take this shift and let me get a couple hours' shut-eye, I can take him on."

"We got him, brother. You go crawl into bed and sleep." Kirby walked around the island and gripped Oscar's shoulder, rocking him back and forth. "Congratulations on being the baby whisperer and all that, but you're beat, man. Go get some sleep."

He yawned again, ending on a stretch. "Yeah, yeah. Wake me when you need to."

***

It didn't matter that he knew it was a dream. He could tell his dream self that it wasn't real a thousand times, and it still felt like he was right back in the middle of a war zone.

The unmistakable whistle of an incoming round split the air, and he watched as the men around him ran for the bunkers near the center of the base they called Mortaritaville. Bent double, heads up while making themselves as small a target as possible, they raced towards the dirt-and-sandbag reinforced holes they'd been told to occupy during moments like this. He'd heard it called the pucker factor, a level of terror that took a body over when danger was imminent. A measure of how tight it made a body's sphincter, and how a soldier handled themselves through it. Growing up, his Pops had told him more than once that a man couldn't manufacture courage. It wasn't a thing that could be awarded or trained. Had reassured him that feeling terror didn't make him less of a man. Pops' words of wisdom stated that courage was pushing through to do the needed thing even if he was terrified.

He sure wasn't feeling courageous right now. Oscar wanted to follow the men, he needed to, but his body wouldn't cooperate, feet as heavy as if they were fitted with cement shoes and stuck in molasses. A nearby boom, striking with a bone-rattling concussion, said the insurgents hadn't found their range yet. That one had hit short of the camp. Oscar could see the dust rising in the air from what was no doubt a collapsed building. It didn't matter that they hadn't hit their target, since according to them, it was the privilege of those townspeople who'd just died to help the cause and take out as many infidels as possible.

Another whistling racket started, growing louder by the second, and he watched as the mortar exploded against a building just to the side of the camp. More a waystation than a true camp, but with the bunkers, this posting felt slightly more permanent. The flash and boom were immediate, a wave of hot air nearly knocking him off his feet, and he swayed into the wind, eyes narrowed protectively against the ash and soot.

The whistling started again, coming from a distance and growing closer. Oscar looked up in time to see the ordnance coming in, aimed directly at his position. He stared, watching as it grew larger and larger until it blotted out everything and was all he could see.

Oscar woke panting, pillow clutched over his head, huddled on his knees in the middle of his mattress. *Fuck.* He hadn't dealt with that dream for a long time, not since right after coming back from overseas. It wasn't how things had happened, not quite. He'd been crouched alongside a building waiting for his chance to run to supposed safety when the bunker had taken a direct hit from enemy fire. The mortar had exploded upon impact, tearing the entrance out of the ground and scattering shrapnel in a wide radius.

Regardless that there were more incoming rounds, he and a handful other soldiers had immediately gone to rescue anyone who could be. It was a miracle that no one died, but two of the men sheltering inside had been injured so badly they'd lost limbs to amputation.

The incident had been two years before he separated from the service and had been a scene he'd never wanted to see played out again. *At least I got that wish.*

He evaluated the chances of falling back asleep without dreaming, shook his head, and swung his legs over the edge of the mattress, squinting at his phone. Two hours until sunrise, and it was January in Northeast Texas, which meant a level of cold that ruled out working in the backyard. He could go for a ride, and often would, ignoring the stiffness brought on by the windchill, but he wanted to be close today, and if he got on the bike, he could get lost in his head and disappear for hours.

As he sat trying to decide how his day would go, the screen on his phone lit up with an incoming call. Local number, which could mean anything, so he scooped it up.

"Yeah?"

"Oscar?" He didn't recognize the female voice, but he made a noise of acknowledgment. "It's Kristie at the hospital. Lindsay Ashworth's asking after you. Deb left your number with a note that you were Ms. Ashworth's local contact."

Before she finished speaking, he was on his feet and reaching for his jeans. "What's wrong?"

"Nothing's wrong, Oscar. She had a bad dream and woke up asking about you. I can patch you through to the phone in her room if you'd like."

"Nope. I'm right here in town. I'll be there in just a few minutes. Tell her I'm coming, okay?" Two steps to the dresser and he yanked open a drawer, tugging out a clean shirt. "I'll be right there." Without giving the woman a chance to respond, he disconnected and tossed the phone to the nightstand, where it rattled against his keys.

Two minutes later, he was out the door and striding along the sidewalk, his brisk walk just this side of a trot.

Chapter Four
Lindsay

Stretched out on her side at the edge of the bed, she stared down into the bassinette, trailing her fingers along Christopher's body. The gentlest of touches, she'd occasionally press her palm against his chest, just to feel him breathing. It had taken a long time to calm herself, but finally her lids were drooping.

The door opening startled her, and she pushed up on an elbow to turn and look, surprised to find Oscar slipping into the darkened room. The instrument panels gave off more than enough glow to see his face, and it looked like he was smiling.

"Hey," he called out softly, his mouth going back to that relaxed smile.

"Oscar." Pleased to see him, she didn't try to hide it and knew he'd picked up on it when his soft smile turned into a grin with a flash of teeth in his beard. "Come see, he's sleeping." As he made his way around the bed to where the bassinette was, she pushed back and up along the mattress, making room for him to sit alongside her hips. As with everything that had happened during Christopher's birth, it felt natural and right to give Oscar this space at her side. She didn't worry about her instinctive reaction, didn't question it. "Isn't he gorgeous?"

"Handsome fella, that's a fact." He did the same thing she had, his palm flattened across Christopher's chest and belly, his fingers wrapping around a tiny shoulder. "He's sleepin' good."

"Yeah," she cooed, adjusting to rest her head on the pillow. She split her attention between the sleeping babe and the man staring down at him with an expression of such gentle pride and affection that it took her breath away. "He's up every couple of hours to feed but sleeps well in between."

"Hard work fighting to get to air." His fingers stroked, adjusting a fold on the blanket wrapped tightly around Christopher. "Wears a body out." He turned his head and looked at her. "How about you? Don't look like you're sleeping between times. You restin' like you should?"

"As I can." She shook her head against the pillow. "I had a bad dream and can't...I haven't been able to get back to sleep."

"Burdens are easier shared, even unreasonable ones. Tell me about your dream." He shifted, cocking one knee on the mattress so it pressed against her in an oddly comforting way. The heat of his body soaked through the sheet separating them. "I got all the time you need."

"I—I... It's silly."

"So?" he shot back. "Just 'cause you think it's silly don't mean it isn't stealin' your rest away. Talk it out, we'll sort it out, and you'll be back to restin' easy, Lindsay."

"Lindy." She smiled at him. "My friends always used to call me Lindy."

"Honored." There was so much emotion in that single word she blinked and stared at his face, which had turned a flinty kind of hard that told her it meant something to him that she'd given him that name. "Now, tell me, Lindy."

"Okay." She paused, but he didn't recant his offer, so she dived in. "I was here, like I am now. I think that's why it felt so real, because part of it is, you know?" He nodded but didn't speak, and she tipped her head back to stare up at the darkened ceiling. "I woke up and a man was standing next to Christopher, had his hand on the bassinette. Not the baby's—" Even stopping short of saying the word that haunted her, it still made guilt prick her eyes with hot tears knowing her poor judgement in men had set the start of Christopher's life on a fatherless track. *I want Oscar to like me. What would he think if he knew?* Lindsay tried to pick back up, changing direction to hide her fears. "—not anyone that I know. But he started spouting off gibberish legalese, and all I could do was stare at him. He finished, then backed towards the door, but he did it taking my son with him." She took a deep breath. "I screamed and cried, asking him why he would do this to me. To my son. He told me it was in the best interests of the child, that I didn't have anything to offer. I couldn't get up. It was like I'd been glued to this bed. So all I could do was ask him not to as he went away. The door closed and it was dark in here, so dark I couldn't see anything, couldn't feel anything, and I prayed I was dead. I knew a life without Christopher wasn't something I'd survive. I prayed and prayed, and then I woke up and the nurse was standing over Christopher, and I... I kinda freaked out."

She didn't realize Oscar had moved until his hand brushed her face. The contact wasn't startling, it was comforting as the heat and weight of his touch steadied her. She leaned into it, feeling his thumb sweep her cheek, gliding through the wet streaming from her eyes.

"That had to be terrifyin', Lindy. But it's not going to happen. It was just a bad dream, you know that, right? You're a good momma, anyone looking at you can see that. And you'll do what you need to in order to provide for your boy." His voice was by turns stern and gentle, and she liked that nearly as much as she liked his touch. "I don't know much about you, but I'm a good judge of character. There's nothing about you that tells me anything except you're a good person who wound up in a bad situation, and that doesn't define who you are. Who you are is that good person. I know that down in my gut. So don't you worry about any bad dream. Put it right out of your head, and focus on what you need to do, what you need next. We'll get you where you need to be." His voice went from stern to steel when he told her, "I promise you that."

It was like he tried to lay every fear to rest at once. Gathering them up in his words, folding them into tiny pieces until they weren't threatening anymore. *Oscar's a special man*. She knew he'd understand, so on a whisper, she shared, "I'm so scared."

His touch never wavered, thumb stroking gently across her cheek, fingers curved around the back of her neck, and he stared into her face, the expression on his resolute. "I know you are," he whispered back, no less intense for the quiet. "You've got a little baby, a helpless being who depends on you for everything. Brought a life into this world, and that's the most beautiful thing I've ever seen, watching you see him for the first time, hold him for the first time, become the momma you were meant to be. So you let yourself be his momma, and then you've got to let me help you with the rest. I'll make it so you aren't scared anymore, at least not for the same things." His lips pressed tightly together, then split in a small smile. "There's plenty of scary things in this world. I've seen my share. But you bein' who you were meant to be, mothering that boy? That's so far from scary it's not even in the same country. That's making your own territory, and ownin' it. You just gotta let me help you now so you can find your way."

"I live in a motel," she told him, voice trembling even as she tried to firm it. Hard enough to admit her failings in the silence of her own head, it was twice as difficult to say these things aloud. "I don't have a job, not now. Why would they wait for me when they need what they need now? Freelancers are a dime a dozen."

"I have a house, and it's got a pair of bedrooms I'm not usin'. You give me your room key, and I'll move everything you have today."

Lindsay sat silent, stunned at the offer. *He doesn't even know me.* She thought back to how Deb and the doctor had spoken to Oscar, with respect and deference, showing through every interaction the kind of man they believed him to be. What'd he'd said about Christopher struck true, creating another well of fear inside her. Her tiny newborn was depending on her to make all the right decisions, to keep him safe. This seemed an offer that was too good to be true. She blinked wet away. "It can't be that easy."

"It's as easy as you let it be, Lindy." His smile was wider, more confident now. "Easy as you let me make it."

"You don't have to—" She paused when he shook his head firmly. "Oscar, you don't. I can... I can figure out something."

"There's a sayin' about savin' a life and becoming responsible for that life, you know that one?" She nodded, frowning at Oscar's abrupt topic change. "I think there's another one that says when you're part of bringing a new life into the world, however that happens, there's a responsibility for that life. That's what I'm asking for, Lindy. You let me take this on, because I need it just as much as you do."

She stared at him, seeing for the first time the dark circles under his eyes, the shadowed expression. He looked like a man who sat in the grip of something regularly, and that something wasn't good. Then she remembered his kindness, his care of her during Christopher's birth, how he'd looked staring down at her son. And just now, how he'd somehow known she needed a friend and had walked into her hospital room without giving it a second thought, being there when she was at her lowest.

Okay, she thought. *Okay*. Carefully choosing her words, she told him, "If I let you take that on—take me on like you're talking about—then you need to know it goes both ways. If you're responsible for me in any way, I'm responsible for you, too. You're a good man, Oscar Mayhan. Deb spoke highly of you, as have the other nurses. I get the feeling that no matter my answer, you'd be doing what you wanted anyway." He grinned at that, giving her an indication she'd read him right, and she gave him the same, surprised when his expression gentled at her smile. "So, if we do this, it's going to have to be a give-and-take, because I can't accept charity. Not for me."

"For your boy, you would," he shot back, and she sighed because he was right. His grin told her he knew it, too. Oscar sobered and studied her for a moment, and she felt the approving weight of his gaze. "But it's not charity. I work for a foundation, and we need some marketing assistance. I also have a cousin down at the Chamber, and I'll call her tomorrow—today." He laughed quietly. "See what they'll work out for you. My house has three bedrooms, but because I don't like being alone much, I stay with friends a lot of the time. You and Christopher won't be putting me out at all. Promise."

"Then... okay." She closed her eyes, taking in the feel of his comforting touch, the presence at her side that felt so solid, and the promise of a stable place to be for a while alongside the possibility of work. "Okay."

Christopher made a snuffling sound, and she quickly looked to where he lay. Swaddled as he was in the hospital's blue blanket, her baby stretched, yawned hugely, and mewled like a kitten, tiny and weak. She lost the heat and pressure of Oscar's touch but got to watch this big man, this strong man, this unbelievably kind man, hover over the bassinette with hands out, clearly at a loss as to how to pick up a baby.

Lindy laughed for the first time in a long time at that.

***

Cradling Christopher to her breast, she stared in awe as the discharging nurse showed her all the things in the hospital's "welcome to motherhood" gift basket. Multiple packages of diapers and wipes, infant medication, tiny baby nail clippers, a bulb thingie for if he got stuffy... There was a wardrobe in packages of onesies, socks, hats, mittens, a sleeper sack, shirts and pants, and a dozen other things. She determinedly ignored the nurse's surreptitious efforts to scrape off the price tags from some of the things, something that told Lindy not every mother had the same wealth bestowed on her. She waited until the nurse had packed things that would fit back inside a diaper bag that was the basket part of the gift, had bagged up all the things that wouldn't, and was smiling down at Christopher before she said, "Tell everyone thank you for the impromptu baby shower. I love it all."

The wrinkled nose and grin told her the message of gratitude had been received and would be passed along.

She'd never met as friendly and kind a group of people in her life. Not just the nurses, but the doctors, and even the admitting woman who'd been eating lunch when Lindy showed up at the hospital. It seemed everyone had trailed in at some point to *oooh* and *aaah* over Christopher.

Oscar had been back every few hours, whatever job he did for that foundation giving him ample leeway in attendance to allow for frequent breaks. He'd brought in his cousin Kirby and Kirby's fiancée, Dana, another person associated with the foundation she'd learned supported combat-wounded veterans. Oscar had introduced her to Nathan and his wife, Cathy, who'd promised Lindy she and Dana had made the guest room at Oscar's house an oasis Lindy would love. Having been raised in a metropolitan suburb, she quickly decided there was something to be said for small towns where everyone knew everybody else. When there was a need, it seemed like everyone pitched in. There'd even be a crib waiting, given to them by the mayor no less, a man who turned out to be Oscar's second cousin.

Her job for the city was secure; they'd told Oscar to tell her congratulations and to not worry about a thing, the deposit they'd paid standing as surety that she'd complete the work. Kirby's plans for the charitable foundation were exciting, and Lindy couldn't wait to dig in and put together a campaign for him, something he'd said would be waiting for her when she felt ready to begin.

Oscar stuck his head in around the door, dazzled her with a smile, and asked the nurse, "Hey, Donna. She ready to go?"

Lindy smiled and gave him a little wave, answering for herself. "Yes, she's ready."

"Hey." He stepped around the nurse and to her side, bending close to touch Christopher's hand. The little boy's fingers immediately wrapped around Oscar's fingertip, and his next greeting was for her son. "Hey, Chris. How's my big boy today?" The door sighed shut behind Donna, leaving Lindy with Oscar.

Rolling her eyes, she reminded him of her preference. "Christopher."

"Lind*say*." He drawled her name out long. "If you think this boy's teachers and friends are gonna stick with that long name, you're full of it." He angled his head to catch her gaze with his and smiled, then made his point, "Lindy."

She felt a touch, and instead of continuing the teasing argument, she looked down at Christopher to see Oscar's hand had shifted and now rested against her as well. He had been careful to not make her feel awkward about their rushed and somewhat exposed introduction, which meant she knew this was inadvertent contact, so she jostled her bundled baby, unseating his fingers from the curve of her breast as blood rushed to her face.

"You ready to go home?" The casual way he said it made tears well in her eyes.

If only I'd met someone like Oscar instead of— She cut off her thoughts, unwilling to even name the man in her mind. She blinked away the threatening tears and looked up, waiting until he dragged his gaze from Christopher to her. *He deserves to understand.*

"Do you know how much it means to me that you care? A stranger." She lifted a hand to stall his interruption, waiting until he closed his mouth, lips thinning resolutely in a way that told her he'd have his say afterwards. "A stranger in profound need, and you've done everything in your power to help. And now, you're inviting a single mother with a newborn into your home, knowing the schedule my son keeps is an every-two-hours one. You've moved my things, organized your friends to help, and introduced me to them so I'd have a larger circle of my own contacts here in town. You secured my current freelance project and expanded that to include a new client."

She leaned forwards, arching over Christopher. "And I know you'll say it's nothing, or say anyone would do the same, but you're wrong. You're wrong, and I hope you never know how wrong, but I'll share a tiny thing today so you'll know how much it means to me that you're taking me in. My son's father wanted to give me a few hundred dollars to handle what he saw as a problem. He made it clear that if I kept the baby, he would have no part of it, having offered the only support he could find it inside himself to give. I chose so wrongly, it's not even funny, and looking back I see things clearly now. That should make me not trust people, not trust men. But you're the exception, Oscar Mayhan. You're special, and such a gorgeous human being inside and out, and I hope to God that you know it. If you don't know it, then take one thing from this. I hope you take away that you're unique, and I'm blessed to know you. Me and Chris"— she'd hoped for a break in his intense expression, but using the shortened name for her son didn't earn anything, so Lindy forged ahead—"we're blessed that you were behind that desk, that you stepped in and made yourself a place in our lives, and that in doing so, you've given us a place in yours. You're our hero." Reaching out, she gripped Oscar's hand and shook it back and forth. "Thank you, Oscar. Thank you."

He didn't speak, didn't move, but his fingers clutched tightly around hers. She unfolded her crossed legs, slipped over the side of the bed and stood in front of him, looking up. Oscar stared straight ahead, and for a moment, she didn't think he saw her at all. Then his body jerked and he tipped his chin down, gaze directed straight towards her. They stood like that for a minute, then he pulled in a hard, ragged breath that shook his frame.

Voice low and quietly intense, he told her, "You're giving me more than you know, Lindy. It'll be good to have company in the house, and you trusting me like you are, that's a gift, too. Something I needed." He lifted their joined hands and wrapped hers around Christopher, then brushed his thumb along the baby's face, gentle as a butterfly's wing. "He deserves to have the best start we can give him, and I'm blessed we can approach that goal together." His head came up, hand falling back to his side as he took a step away, something she didn't like but couldn't put her finger on why, and said, "Now we're done talking our heads off, let's get you two home. My truck's parked downstairs, and I've got the car seat already installed." He leaned sideways and dragged a wheelchair she hadn't noticed closer. "Hop on in, little momma. Let's get you home."

***

Oscar

The recliner in the living room was comfortable and familiar, as were the pictures on the wall, the rug on the floor, and even the late afternoon sunshine streaming through the window.

Oscar leaned his head back, settling deeper into the chair as he made a list of the unfamiliar. Baby powder scent, the creak of a rocker in the other room, and the soft hum of a woman's voice as she sang soothingly to her babe in arms. His chest warmed, a feeling of contentment settling over him.

She'd called him her hero. Said it and meant it, deep down to her soul. He'd seen the honesty of the statement in her eyes.

Oscar had loved it, her whole speech, because he felt the same way, only about her.

He was blessed to have had the honor of being there when her child was born. That, and the hours leading up to that glorious culmination of all her work, had changed him in ways he still hadn't cataloged. Blessed to have friends to help out, to know people to talk to on her behalf, blessed to have a place custom-made for her to recover and have her babe thrive. Blessed to know her, no matter the secrets she was still holding close.

From what little she'd shared, he understood how terrified she'd been throughout her whole pregnancy. When her job came to an end, the car and apartment that had been part of her compensation package ended, too. She'd been ousted, no insurance, jobless and homeless, and trying to do the best she could. The junker he'd driven over and parked inside the garage was not worth the money it'd take to fix it up, but he had a line on a car for her. She wouldn't need one for a while, but he'd make sure what she had was safe for her and Christopher.

The baby cried out, soft and low, more vocalizing than distress, and he smiled. That was something whoever the jackhole was would never have, that evidence of the miracle of life. *Throwing money at her for an abortion and absolving himself of any responsibility?* Oscar didn't understand how any man could do that and was glad he didn't, because it meant he had a heart. Family was family, and when you made a miracle, you didn't turn your back on that, no matter how hard things got.

He and Kirby had grown up with a big family, and it wasn't until he was in his twenties that he realized not everyone was connected by blood. It didn't matter. Their grandfather had been one of thirteen kids, all of them his uncles and aunts, and their children his cousins. The family tree was twisted and took interesting turns, because his grandfather and the two oldest were full siblings. Their mother had died, and their father remarried a woman who had two kids, their step-siblings. The couple then had five kids together, their half-siblings. Their father had died, and their step-mother had remarried a man who had a child, and they then had two children together. Thirteen kids, raised side by side as blood, no matter the actual relationship. As far as Oscar was concerned, that's what family did, and that's what family was.

So to him, it didn't matter that Christopher had a father out there who wasn't in the picture. The picture right now was Lindy, and him, because he'd adopted them sure as anything, following the tradition passed down through the family.

Family wasn't limited to what genes you shared.

Family was something you made out of what you were given.

Chapter Five
Lindsay

She sat up in bed, startled by whatever had woken her, and listened closely. Chris slept quietly. His tiny breaths in and out reassured her that he was okay. She shook her head and had decided to lie back down when she heard a low groan through the walls of the house. *Oscar.*

Reacting to the anguished sound, she bolted from the bed and left the door open behind her, hand on Oscar's bedroom door a moment later. She heard a muttered, "Fucking hell," tortured and rough, and didn't pause, throwing the door open wide. Light seeped in through his windows. Oscar was on his back, bare chested, tangled in the covers, head thrown to the side. Eyes closed, his face was twisted, mouth open in a silent scream.

"Oscar?" He thrashed at the sound of her voice, his moves violent and uncoordinated. "Oscar, are you okay?"

"Fucking hell," he muttered again, chin lifting as his back bowed. "Fuck them all to hell."

Lindy hovered beside the bed for a moment, then caught his hand as it flailed near, his fingers nearly crushing hers as he took hold. "I'm here," she told him, and his face turned to her, seeking, with eyes still closed. "You're not alone." Her worst fear, and the thing she held close from his words two weeks ago when he'd brought her home. Home, here, where he was caught in the grips of some nightmare she couldn't understand. "You're home, Oscar. Home."

His grip tight, he pulled her towards him, unbalancing her so she fell to the mattress beside him. Oscar immediately turned and wrapped his arms around her, hauling her against his chest, throwing a leg over and hooking it behind her knee to tangle them together. His heart raced, beating so hard even in the uncertain lighting she could see how it thudded against his ribs. *He's done so much for me, for us. I'd do anything to make this better for him.* She relaxed into his hold, giving him her weight, and she felt him take in a deep breath, then blow it out slowly.

"You're okay, Oscar. I'm here." All she could do was reassure him, and she did that repeatedly, continuing until his muscles relaxed and his heartbeat slowed, until his breathing came normally again. Still, he held tight to her, and when she tried to pull away, he made such a distressed sound as he clasped her close that she didn't try again for a long time. She'd give anything to have this be hers, a place at his side like this, where she had a right to comfort him. *I'll take what I can get.* "I'm here. You're okay."

A couple of hours later, Chris snuffled himself awake in the other room, and as his first cry hit the air, Oscar tensed in a different way. His question was rough, rumbling through him as he asked, "Lindy?"

"Shhh." She pushed back, and he let her this time, reluctantly it seemed, but he let her go. "Go back to sleep, Oscar. It was just a dream."

"You're my dream," he muttered, turning his face into the pillow.

She stared down at him for a moment, then turned to go care for her son.

Chapter Six
Oscar

Sweat prickled along the back of his neck as he rolled away from the door and shoved his hand underneath the pillow. Another dream had woken him, but not a bad one this time. He'd had enough of those to last a lifetime, memories stretched like taffy by his subconscious so even the most innocent of conversations were fodder for the demons that populated his dreams. They'd slowed, nearly stopping in the month since Lindy moved in with Chris, only plaguing him once a week or so.

He knew Lindy had a lot to do with that. Always when the dreams were the worst, she'd somehow hear Oscar's restlessness and come sit with him. He'd woken more than once with his head buried in her stomach, arms banded around her, holding on for dear life. She'd stay beside him, losing her own precious rest to help make his a little better.

No, this wasn't one of those dreams.

In this one, Lindy had been in his room, in his bed, but in a very different way. Naked and writhing underneath him, she'd stared into his face as she told him how much she loved him. *Loved me.* Her voice had been low and rough when she said she wanted him. Wanted him inside her.

His cock throbbed, aching, and he had just decided to stroke himself off when he heard the doorknob rattle. *Fuck.*

"Oscar?" Her voice came from beside the door, and he thanked God she hadn't ventured farther into the room.

He rolled up on a hip and twisted to look back at her. "I'm good, Lindy."

"You sure?" Her posture changed, relaxing slightly. "Need me to stay for a bit?"

Shaking his head, he stared at her. Little ruffled nightie, sheer fabric covered with painted-on red poppies, the bottom edge swirled and shimmied around her thighs. Her breasts strained the bodice, and it emphasized that she had curves for days, exactly like he liked her. Beautiful, lush, generous, and giving... Oscar swallowed hard, forced his voice to some semblance of normalcy, and lied through his teeth. "No, Lindy. I'm good."

Hesitating, she shifted on her feet, which set the hem of that nightie twirling around her legs, inches below where he'd love to bury his face. *Fuck*. His cock jerked, and he tried to ignore the need pooling deep in his belly, the promise of electricity strong enough to stiffen all his muscles, if he'd only take hold. If she came to him right now, he wouldn't try to deny himself. *Please*.

"Okay, if you're sure." She took a deep breath, and his mouth watered when he saw her nipples were stiff and hard, poking little pup tents in the material. "Good night, Oscar."

"'Night, baby." Her chin dipped at his response, and he could have sworn the expression that crossed her face was pleased. "See you tomorrow."

She smiled and pulled the door shut behind her, leaving him to his darkened room, alone.

Oscar closed his eyes and lay back on the bed, then snaked a hand down and wrapped his fingers around his dick, stroking firmly as he went back through that encounter again. And again. And again, until he was groaning, hoping like fuck she'd made it back to sleep before she had to hear him come with her name on his lips.

***

Lindsay

"Thank you." She stood from the chair and adjusted Chris in her arms, holding out a hand for the man on the other side of the desk. "I appreciate all your help."

"Not a problem, Ms. Ashworth. Oscar's a good friend. It's nice to see him being taken care of for a change." Nonplussed, Lindsay tipped her head to the side and stared at him. The bank president was Oscar's cousin, but their transaction today hadn't been about Oscar at all, just Lindsay opening a new bank account here in town. "You know how he is, always doing for others. It's just good to see him so happy."

Lindsay's teeth clenched together as what he was implying came clear. Not that she'd be opposed to it, but Oscar had done so much for her and Chris. There was no way she'd take advantage of him that way.

"Mr. Mayhan"—like half the town, he shared Oscar's last name—"I think you've gotten the wrong impression. Oscar and I are friends. Good friends. Roommates. Nothing more." She waggled the envelope of temporary checks he'd just handed over, along with the deposit slip for her first two paychecks from the city and one from the MBMC. "Most of these will be written to cover my rent, paid directly to Oscar. I agree he's a very good man, worthy and sweet, and willing to go the distance for something he believes in." She shook her head. "But we are not involved, if that's what you were implying."

The man studied her a minute, and his gaze fell to the top of his shiny desk, void now of anything to interrupt the expanse of wood. He leaned forwards, fingers propped on the edge, and lifted his eyes to stare directly at her. "No offense meant, Ms. Ashworth. Small towns, you know how it is."

She nodded and thanked him again, turning towards the door.

"Ms. Ashworth?" Lindsay twisted to look back to him, Chris heavy in her arms. "You seem like a nice lady, and I know a lot of people here in town already think the world of you." She stared at him, unsure where this was going. "I hear you're smart, good at your job, quick to compliment folks, and you look at Oscar like he's your whole world." She froze in place, heart rabbiting in her chest at his words that cut too close to her secret. "And smart as you are, if you can't see he looks at you the same way, maybe you're right and there's nothing there." He stepped back, angled into his chair, and gave her a brief nod. "Good to meet you."

Chris started fussing, and Lindsay stroked his back automatically, staring at the man for a final moment before she walked away.

***

Oscar

"No, man. It's not like that." He bent to pull a skillet from underneath the counter, angling up to see Kirby and Brian staring at him. They were at the clubhouse, and it was Oscar's turn to cook for the members. He'd already traded favors with the guys more than once to cover his shift. It was time to just man up and do his part. "She's not into me like that."

"Oh, Jesus. You got a serious case of the blinders." Brian chuckled and lifted a bottle to his mouth, draining the water in a long gulp. "Should we tell him, Kirby?"

Oscar shook his head as he dragged a container of hamburger out of the refrigerator. "There's nothing to tell me, so you might as well give it up." The huge stockpot of water was already boiling, steam rising from the bubbling surface. He rifled through the cabinet until he found the spices he needed for the meat, then dug through the refrigerator again for a tub of butter. "She's just not into me. A man knows."

"Hey, Donny!" Kirby's yell echoed through the building. "Who do you think Lindy's sweet on?"

"Ain't no thinkin', brother. She's all about that Oscar, man." Donny was still talking as he and Walt walked into the kitchen. "Oh, s'getti. That's some good eats. I'll get the garlic bread out."

"She's not sweet on me." Oscar stared down at the slowly browning meat, stirring it with a spatula. *Wish like fuck she was.* "Drop it, man." Their teasing had never held an edge of cruelty before, no matter the topic, and Oscar hated showing them how this mattered, but he couldn't deal if they continued in this vein. The anger rolling through him felt foreign, not something he wanted to give a place to stick to. Through clenched teeth, he pushed out, "Just fuckin' drop it."

Silence fell in the room, broken by shuffling feet and smothered coughs. Without turning around, he reached for the box of noodles, breaking several handfuls in half and dropping them into the boiling water.

"Oscar, we didn't mean—"

He cut Kirby off with a jerk of his head. "Don't worry about it."

A hand fell on his shoulder and squeezed. "Food smells good." Brian offered a graceful change of subject that Oscar hoped the other men grabbed onto with both hands.

Donny followed suit, asking, "What can I do to help?"

"Table." The one word was all Oscar could grit out.

"You got it." Another hand gripped his shoulder, then another, and the men filed past him, leaving Oscar alone in the kitchen.

If only.

***

"How are the dreams?" Dominic Reed's voice was soft, soothing, something Oscar figured took a lifetime to perfect.

Oscar rolled his neck, satisfied when it drew two sharp pops from the tense muscles as he tried to decide how to answer the question from the foundation-provided counselor. One of the requirements for membership was at least a twice monthly chat with the man, which normally Oscar minded a fuck of a lot, because it seemed a waste of resources on him. Today, it felt like more of a process and less of an imposition.

"They're dreams, man. Nothing to get bent out of shape about." He shrugged. "They're somewhat better."

"Because of Lindy." Not a question, Dom's statement backed up things Oscar had let slip in the previous weeks. He made an agreeable noise. "Does she know what happened to you overseas?"

"What? Nothing happened to me. I did my tours and came home." His shrug was less comfortable, not fitting as well, muscles across his shoulders binding his movements. "Nothing to talk about."

"Tell me why you don't like talking to me." The abrupt topic change shook Oscar's confidence, and he dropped his gaze from the corner of the ceiling to Dom's face. "And don't deny it. The truth is plain as day, every time we chat."

"Well, maybe we talk too damn often, then." He shifted in the chair, cushions too plush for his liking today. "I'd be good with once a quarter, Dom. I'm good, man."

"What's your definition of courage?"

Unsettled, he stared at Dom for a moment, then shook his head. Ignoring the man wouldn't gain him anything, so he delivered the bare minimum to answer the question. "Doing what's needed, no matter what."

"Are you courageous?"

"What? Fuck, man. Where's this going?" He leaned forwards, propping elbows on knees. "I'm just doin' my job."

"Were you doing your job when you pulled those men from a burning bunker?" Oscar froze, the remembered scent of explosives wafting past his nostrils, bitter and pungent. "Running into the open while the base was still under bombardment and going into a hole in the ground to try and save their lives?" The chair shook underneath him, vibrations from distant mortar round strikes rocking it back and forth. "That wasn't your job. But you did it anyway."

With effort Oscar pulled his gaze away from Dom's face, ignoring the gentle concern in his expression. "Anyone would have done the same."

"False. Out of nearly two dozen men, you were the first to move. Alone. When you pulled the first man out, you begged for help, and got it, from three more men. But it was you. If you hadn't gone in when you did, every one of those men in the bunker would have died." Something obscured Oscar's vision, burning and watery. "I've listened to you for months now. Months where you dodged the reality of what happened, what it cost you. It's time to face the music, Oscar. What happened and all that you saw, it marked you, just as much as if you'd been hit yourself."

Ducking his head, his words were aimed at the floor. "I just did what was right. What anyone would have done."

"Anyone with courage. Courage is doing what's needed, even if you're about to shit yourself with fear. That's the definition of courage, and you are a goddamned hero, Oscar Mayhan." Dom's chair scooted closer, his hand landing on Oscar's arm, holding fast, anchoring him. "Those medals you don't like? They tell the truth. You just have to figure out a way to accept it."

"Lindy... Man, she's so brave." Throat tight, he forced the words out. "Doesn't matter what it is, she hits it head on. She's the one with courage."

"Let her share that with you, then. Whatever you two are doing in that house you used to hate is working, Oscar. If that's you sharing her courage to face the dreams, then keep on keepin' on. I like seein' you without ghosts in your eyes, and I'm proud of the work you've done. But—" Dom drew a deep breath. "You gotta tell her what she's helping you with. Give that to her. From what I've seen, she's strong enough to hold it for your sake."

Oscar admitted something to Dom he'd been trying to ignore. "I like her, Dominic. I like her a lot."

"There's a lot there to like." Now the counselor's voice sounded amused, and Oscar glanced at him to see a tiny smile on his lips. "Let's explore that next week, shall we?"

"Fuck you." Oscar's laugh was weak, but it was there. "I won't be exploring that with you anytime soon."

Chapter Seven
Oscar

"I got him." He pushed up from the recliner, a piece of furniture that had seen more use in the past five months than in the two years previous. Chris was snuffling himself awake, the sounds from the baby monitor sweet and soft, slowly gaining volume in a way that Oscar knew if the boy continued down that path, he'd be wide awake and yelling for attention in a couple of minutes.

Glancing to where Lindy was seated at the desk he'd moved into the living room, he noted her posture—bent over her sketchbook, arm moving swiftly as she drew out whatever was in her head, concentrating. "Back in a minute," he called, and she nodded, then lifted her gaze to him, and he felt that look in his gut, something that had been happening more and more often.

"Thank you, Oscar. I'm nearly done. Just a couple of minutes and I'll be in to nurse him." The corner of her mouth lifted in a crooked smile. "He sounds hungry."

"You get set up on the couch. I'll bring him to you," Oscar bartered, gaze on her mouth, because that smile did it for him every fucking time. "We'll watch something."

When he was here while she was working, he kept the TV off. Not at her request, but he'd noted how it jacked with her attention to have a show playing in the background. He'd wanted to put the desk in the guest bedroom, give her a private place to work, but she said she'd already kicked him out of one room in his house, and taking over another didn't seem right. He'd tried to argue, but she'd given him that crooked smile and a "please" and he'd been a goner. He'd stuck to his guns about one thing, refusing to put her office setup in the bedroom she shared with Chris, instead making room here in the living room. After thinking about it, he realized it guaranteed him seeing more of her, and while he'd pushed that ulterior motive to the back of his mind, it was there.

Swinging through the door and into the bedroom, he schooled himself to look away from the nightgown tossed over the foot of her bed. Still, it burned into his brain, like it always did. Something Dana had bought Lindy as a present, it was silky and a soft baby-blue color he knew looked good on her, the bodice and hem ruffled. Instead, he focused on the crib, where Chris had rolled to his stomach, glaring at Oscar through the bars that kept him secure, his sleepy head wobbling back and forth. "Ah," he yelled, mouth open wide. "Gah."

"I got you, kiddo." Oscar soothed Chris with a touch, ending with a soft caress of his head, still covered with its dark cap of thick hair so much like his mother. "I got you." An expert baby wrangler now, the baby whisperer his brothers still called him, Oscar scooped the boy up and set him to his shoulder, still stroking up and down his back. "There, now. How's that?" Fist curled into Oscar's tee, Chris cuddled close, and Oscar loved how that always made him feel. This moment was why he argued for the chance to get Chris up after a nap. "Sleepy baby snuggles are the best." The boy made a quiet sound, and Oscar chuckled, taking it as agreement. "Yeah, you know it, kid." He moved to the changing table, out of experience keeping a hand on the boy as he gathered things necessary for a fresh diaper. By the end, Chris' demands had grown louder, muffled by the way he chewed on his fists between impatient shouts. "Come on, boy, let's go find Momma."

He heard, "Momma's right here," and turned to see Lindy leaning against the doorframe. "My boys were taking a while, so I thought I'd check on them."

Oscar tried not to react to her calling him one of her boys, throwing a barrier around that feeling, fencing it securely in a way she'd never know what it meant.

He was a goner for her, he knew. It hadn't taken long. *Hell, I was half in love with her by the time she came home from the hospital.* But seeing her with Chris, with Oscar's friends, watching her blossom under their attention and affection, laughing with the girls, listening somberly to the stories his brothers told—it had all uncovered a strength and sweetness inside her that he'd found himself drawn to, fighting all the way.

"Chris..." He nuzzled gently into the boy's neck, making him giggle softly at how his whiskers tickled. "Momma's keepin' tabs on us, son." He nuzzled again, getting a head bobble that ended with a face-plant, Chris tucked tight to his chest, fist wrapped up in Oscar's shirt. "Come on, let's get you fed."

Lindy looked up at him, expression soft, that damned crooked smile in place, and asked, "You want me to take him?"

Oscar shook his head, then gave her a chin lift she took as instruction, turning and walking down the hallway in front of him. All of which gave him a gorgeous view to keep in his mind, her hair, body, ass, and sway already enough to keep him up at night, but he didn't mind taking it all in one more time.

"I finished my preliminary ideas for the Mayhan Bucklers fundraiser campaign," she called over her shoulder, head turned just enough he got a flash from her eyes. "You think Kirby would want to see it soon?"

"I think if he knew you had something to look at, he'd make time for you right now. Want me to call him?" He wasn't kidding, either. He and Kirby had taken one gander at the work she'd done for the city and realized they had exactly what they needed in Lindy with her unique way of looking at things. She was artistic, sure, but it was more than that. Even to Oscar's untrained eye, her work was inspired in a way that made it clear this was her calling, not just a job. "This for the charity run?" He got another flash of her eyes and a nod, this coming with a sideways grin. Her growing confidence was good to see, and he chuckled when he asked, "He's gonna love it, isn't he?"

"I hope so. I really, really like what I've put together, but the vision has to match what you guys see for the club." She swung around the end of the couch and sat, settling into position by leaning against the corner cushions. Chris recognized the process and had his head up and watching, starting to yell in earnest. Oscar jostled his arms to distract the boy and watched her from the corner of his eye. She executed the familiar movements to tug at her top and adjust her underthings, and Oscar saw her stretch her arms up for Chris. As he always did, he tried to focus on her face as he handed over the baby, watching the smile he claimed as his appear, cheeks lifting and face growing soft as she looked at her son. "Hey, baby boy. Did you have a good nap?"

Oscar straightened, going to his recliner, where he elevated the footrest and grabbed the remote. "Whatcha wanna watch? Cooking show or that yard one you like?" He flipped on the TV and automatically adjusted the volume down, keeping it quiet to not distract Chris from what he was doing. "Somethin' else today?"

"What do you want to watch?" Lindy's tone was soft, nearly crooning as she settled Chris.

He didn't turn away from the TV, staring straight ahead. If he saw, he'd want, and with her only feet away, she'd see. He couldn't risk ruining the friendship they'd built through the weeks and months.

Her voice was still soft as she called his name like a question, "Oscar?"

"What?" Thumb to the channel button on the remote, he scrolled up through the numbers. "This one's about backyard playgrounds."

"If we weren't here—"

That terrifying statement got his attention, and he looked at her, feeling struck dumb by the beauty he saw.

Lindy was gorgeous, so pretty, and getting more beautiful every day. Chris' dark head cradled to her bare breast was the essence of womanhood, something to be cherished. Him being here, sitting so close while she nursed Chris, made this an intimate moment without having a hint of eroticism. For Oscar, knowing she was nourishing her son, feeding him, keeping him safe and protected in every way, turned it into an act of love. He loved seeing her, being around her, having her and the baby in the house. *She can't leave*. Her words had struck a chord of fear deep inside him. *If they weren't here...* Oscar couldn't imagine a world where he existed without Lindy and Chris.

"What do you mean?" Chris jolted at his barked question. Lindy soothed him with a hand smoothing over the curve of his head, gaze locked on Oscar. He toned it down before he repeated his question, surprised at the confusion on her face. "What do you mean, if you weren't here?"

Understanding dawned, and she dipped her chin, speaking to the top of Chris' head. "I meant to ask what would you watch on TV if we were in our room?" They were both silent for a moment, the muffled sound of some random TV show rolling in the background. "Oscar?" Her voice was low, and it trembled the slightest bit. She didn't look up as she asked, "Is it... Are you ready for us to move out?"

"What? No. Fuck no." His reaction was immediate and earned him her eyes. She cut her gaze up from under a fall of hair, studying him cautiously. "I'll say it straight out. I don't want you to think about leaving. That's what tweaked me." He pushed against the footrest, settling into an upright position, hands on the arms of his chair. "I do not want you to leave, and you can place bets on that, because it's a sure winner."

"I just don't want to overstay my welcome. And you do so much for us."

He didn't do as much for her as he wanted to, but she'd drawn some very clear lines in the beginning. If it was about Chris, she'd accept without grousing too much. Anything for her son, just like a good momma should. When he'd tried to do for her, she wouldn't throw it back in his face, but he'd learned the idea of being a charity case dug deep and hurt her, so he'd stopped. She wanted to earn her way, so he'd set about to do what he could to give her every opportunity for just that. After some trial and error, how he gave to her was watching Chris while she worked or took a meeting, which was no hardship. Or telling her about a conversation he'd overheard at a Chamber meeting, stepping back and watching as she made the contact, set up appointments, and won business through her talent and personality. She didn't need him, and he wasn't shy about making sure she knew it. But leaving him alone in this house? *It'd kill me.*

"I strike you as a man who'd put up with something in my space I didn't want?" Her head moved back and forth, slow to complete the arc. "You think I'm gonna push to have something if I didn't think it was worth it?" Her hand moved over Chris' head in a gentle caress, and she stared at him. "You've seen me with folks when I'm tryin' to get them to see the error of their ways, yeah?" No response, but he knew the answer. "Yeah, you have. You watched me talk Nathan into going for that new prosthesis trial, and you were on hand when Dana and I went head-to-head about her direction on expanding the foundation. I make any bones about what I thought with either of them?"

"Well, no, but—"

"No buts about it, honey." Her face changed subtly at his slip, but he didn't have time to pursue whatever it was. "If I didn't want you and my boy here"—another change, this one more profound, as if she'd been struck a blow she liked—"then we'd have a conversation where I led you there gently, but I'd lead you there. This isn't you being in my space. It's about my space being filled in a good way by the two of you. Meeting you was the best thing to happen to me in a long, long time. Don't take that away from me." He tried to unclench his fingers from the arms of the chair, but until she gave him an indication she'd heard and understood, he couldn't relax an inch. "I don't know how I can be any clearer, Lindy. Don't think you're a burden, because havin' you and Chris here is so far from that it's not even in the same galaxy. It's like there's this whole universe I'd never even seen, filled with wonder. That's you and our boy. You can't take that away. I need the two of you."

Chris was fussing, pressing deep, then pummeling her with his tiny baby fists, and Oscar lost Lindy's gaze when she looked down at the baby. She was still for a moment, then slid him away from her body to adjust her clothing, exposing her other breast as she prepared to shift him around. "Oscar."

"Yeah…Lindy?" He had to catch himself as he did a hundred times a day, needing to call her honey or baby, sweetheart, anything to lay claim to her in the way he wanted. *Mine.*

"My back's aching." Before she finished, he was up and moving towards her. Lindy hitched herself sideways on the couch, making room for him to squeeze in behind her, and he did, shoving himself into the cushions, leaving enough space to use one hand to rub her back. "Thank you," she whispered, slumping a little.

"Any time." They sat like that for a few minutes, sounds of Chris nursing soft and so sweet it made Oscar smile.

"I don't want to go anywhere," she said quietly, and he closed his eyes in relief. "You… Oscar, you're my best friend."

Friend wasn't close to what he wanted, but he'd take what he could get. "Then don't go anywhere." He kept up the massage on her lower back as she half turned to face him. "Stay." Lindy looked up, and he saw her lashes were clumped with tears. "Hey now. No cryin'." Oscar curled his arm around her shoulders, drawing her in to lean against him. "No tears. You wanna be here, and I want that, too. More than you know. It's all copasetic, yeah?"

"Yeah," she muttered against his shoulder, sounding subdued, and he dipped his chin to look at her. Chris' hand rested against his mother's breast, mouth and jaw working as he suckled, and the exposed slope of flesh from her cheek to throat to breast was exquisite in a way that Oscar knew he'd never known beauty until this woman came into his life.

"Lindy."

She glanced up, and her lips parted as she breathed, "Yeah?" There was trust in her gaze, but something else, too. A longing that resonated inside him. A need he suddenly understood.

Oscar angled down, his gaze fixed on those full lips, and she lifted up to meet him in the middle. This first kiss was soft, slow, an exploration he'd wanted to do for months, and when her tongue touched his mouth, he groaned, arm tightening around her shoulder. It was sweet and gentle, and everything he'd anticipated kissing Lindy would be. Lost in the moment, caught up in a dream come true, he took it deeper, and she turned it hotter when she moaned until it was everything he could do to dial it back, cognizant of where they were and what she was doing. Precious cargo in her arms, and he wanted to hold the two of them forever. Oscar broke the kiss off with effort, lifted a hand, and stroked the soft skin of her cheek. She looked dazed, and he waited a beat before telling her his dearest wish. "Stay."

***

"Totally a move." Lindy grazed the underside of Oscar's jaw with her lips, and he felt her mouth move in what had to be a smile as she teased him.

It had been a week since that first kiss, and it had been followed by many more. They were again on the couch, TV playing softly in the background, and Oscar had wedged himself into the corner, Lindy leaning against his chest. Arms around her, this had become his favorite position and piece of furniture in the house. In the past seven days, his recliner was gathering dust whenever she was in the house, on the chance she'd want to come and snuggle with him. Her work, club business, and the requirements of caring for a young infant meant they hadn't gone any faster than necking like teenagers. He'd take her any way he could get her and hadn't made any bones about it when she'd tried apologizing. Her playful like this? *I'll take it all day long.*

"Are you tellin' me you played me, woman?"

She'd just informed him that her backache that day hadn't been real but an opportunity to get his hands on her any way she could. It seemed they'd both been hiding their attraction. On his side, it was definitely more than liked, but even now he was trying to keep the brakes on and go slowly.

"It got me what I wanted, so I'll own that one, yeah." She twisted and grinned up at him, all evidence of the subtle lines of tension she'd carried in recent months gone. "Are you mad?"

"Uh, no." Oscar chuckled, and she gave him another brilliant grin and rested her cheek against his chest. He pressed his lips to the crown of her head, taking in an easy breath filled with nothing but Lindy. "I was bein' a dumbass, so it's good you got my attention."

"I like you, Oscar." Her soft words carried a distinct weight that hit him in the chest, a velvet blow from her that he didn't mind taking.

"That's good, seein' as I'm the same for you." He did a quick mental calculation, evaluated the silence from the baby monitor, and asked, "Chris gonna be down for a bit?" He anticipated her nod, since she'd just nursed their boy and laid him down, but her shiver was an added bit of deliciousness. His voice dipped low as he asked, "Wanna make out?" She nodded again, and when he angled his head to look at her, she was smiling.

He shifted and hauled her up, twisting so he settled her in the couch, and stretched out alongside her. She touched his face, fingertips trailing along the edge of his jaw, ruffling the scruff of his beard. "Since I met you, I thought this was sexy, wanted to play with it." He lifted his chin, inviting more of the same, and she gave it, nails gently scratching at his cheeks. "I like everything about you."

"Lindy, baby." He captured one of her fingertips between his teeth, pretending to growl. "Kiss me."

She stretched, pressed her mouth to his, and he gave her that play for a minute, letting her lead things. Then just as she was heating it up, he took over, slanting his head to take her mouth, tongue spearing inside to duel with hers. By the second renewal of the kiss, her fingers were wound up in his shirt, holding him tight, desperate whimpers escaping from her lips. At the third, her hands were seeking his skin, pushing at his shirt with little fluttering movements.

He wrapped his arm around her, hand cupping her ass, and pulled her tight against him. His cock was hard and throbbing, and he buried his face into her neck and bit off a groaned, "*Fuck*," at the exquisite feel of her body giving when he thrust against her. "Lindy, we gotta slow down."

"Why?" Her cry was breathy, and she curled her arms around him. "Oscar, why?"

"Well...you. There's Chris." Lindy stiffened, and he felt a shove against his chest. "You're—"

"What?" She interrupted him with a cry that sounded less breathy and more pissed. "I'm what, Oscar?

What about Chris? Huh? Or me? I'm a stupid single mother with too much baggage?"

What the fuck?

He angled his chin down to look at her, seeing wet welling in her eyes. They'd had the discussion about past relationships weeks ago, before what they were now building had even been a possibility. He knew all about the cheating doucheturd who had been party to creating Christopher, knew the details of what came next, leaving Lindy fired, with no references and no client list.

For his history recitation, he'd told her about the woman he'd been falling in love with, someone he'd believed felt the same. How he'd been trying to understand why she didn't want to move in together, headed over for a talk, and used his key to enter her apartment only to walk in and find she had a man there. Someone she saw regularly. Someone she *was* in love with and had been trying to make jealous by using Oscar. It'd worked, and he'd strolled into their private celebration following the man popping the question. The rock on her finger had made a mockery of anything Oscar thought they had.

Lindy throwing out the single mother angle told Oscar she wasn't feeling secure. He wanted to take care of her feelings, set her straight right away, no misunderstandings allowed. But talking like she did rode the edge of pissing him off. Instead of giving in to that anger, he pulled her under him, rolling so he trapped her with his body, pushed up on an arm, and stared down at her.

"Shut it." That threatening wet left her eyes instantly, and he saw the way she bowed up at his words. That was good, meant she had hold of the backbone he'd seen in her. He needed a woman not afraid to buck up against him. "It's nothing to do with the state of your ring finger, Lindy. And I'm looking past it, but you callin' Chris baggage like he's an afterthought, even if I know that ain't what you meant. That's gonna burn you later, so latch onto it now and deal, then put it aside." The wounded expression on her face told him she hadn't thought about those words, and that soothed something inside him. Chris was as important a piece of this whole thing as Lindy, and he loved them both. He just had to find a way to make her understand.

"I didn't—"

He cut her off with a shake of his head, curling his fingers around the back of her neck and holding tight. "I know you didn't, that's what I'm sayin'. Just accept your mouth said a stupid and move on." He gave her a squeeze. "You movin' on?" She blinked fast, squeezed her eyes shut, and nodded. "Fuck, you aren't movin' on. Baby, you got things cross-wired in your head. You're seeing your circumstances as a negative, expecting someone, even me, to pile shit on you in response. You hear me the other day?"

Eyes still closed, she shook her head. Not a no, but in confusion.

"I told you what it means to me that you've given me a place in your lives. You and Chris, you mean the world to me, and the idea you'd take him away, think

84

about it happenin' ever, tears a hole in my soul. Don't make yourself less, not in any way. In my mind, you're more than I deserve. More than I could have ever hoped to have in my world, and you're givin' that to me. The trust you have for me, I wouldn't risk that for anything." He gave her a shake, leaned down, and touched his forehead to hers, earning her bright eyes staring up at him. "What I was tryin' to ask and failin' miserably at was how it's not been that long since you had Chris. He's so little yet. We were goin' fast, right here, and I didn't want to hurt you." He brushed his lips across hers. "I never want to hurt you."

She laughed softly, the fragile sound so welcome and sweet he had to close his eyes to experience it, carrying her joy and pleasure down to his gut. "Oh. That's what you were trying to...? Oscar, it's been months."

"Yeah, and I was there. It hurt you a lot, the whole thing. I know there's gotta be a recovery period or something." He kissed her again. "Never, ever gonna hurt you."

"I was cleared for activity weeks ago." She pushed her fingers through his hair, thumb gliding along his cheek just above his beard, back and forth. "Doc said anytime I wanted to get busy, just to make sure 'my man,' his words, took care of me first. You won't hurt me, and I know you never would, Oscar." She held his gaze. "I am all systems go, honey."

He froze, his mind going a dozen directions, then blurted, "I'm not doin' you on the couch for the first time."

She smiled, the corner of her mouth lifting in that crooked grin, and he swooped in for a kiss that lasted minutes. When he pulled back, she whispered, "Take me to bed, then."

***

Lindsay

In his bedroom, door closed, baby monitor quiet on the nightstand, she had a moment of hesitation when Oscar reached for her. Lindy had always been curvy, but that was more pronounced since she'd gotten pregnant and had Chris. Her belly was still rounded from carrying her baby, not having regained all of the muscle tone. And she had dozens of stretchmarks along her hips and stomach. She could call them warrior stripes in her head all she wanted, but what if they turned him off?

He must have sensed her unease, because Oscar stepped close, dropped his mouth next to her ear, and—as he'd done since they'd met—laid to rest every fear she had.

"Right here, right now, whatever you got goin' on in your head, forget it, Lindsay. Everything I see, I want. You're so fuckin' beautiful, and perfect for me. I *like* what you got goin' on, woman, and if you don't believe me—" He gripped her hand and tugged so she was caressing his hard dick through his jeans. "—then trust this. 'Cause this little guy don't lie. He's all kinds of excited to make your acquaintance."

"He's not so little." Voice trembling as much as her fingers were, she stroked the length of him. Knowing he was as into this as she soothed her nerves. "And he does seem very eager."

"So fuckin' eager, baby." Oscar swayed closer, then dropped his head and took her mouth, possessing her again as he kissed her thoroughly. "I want you in my bed. Fuck, I just want you." He stepped back, and she gave his cock a final stroke, watching his corded neck under the edge of his beard when he tipped his head back on a groan. "Goddamn, honey. Got to knock that shit off. My boy'll miss the main event."

Oscar stripped off his shirt, and she reached for him. A shirtless Oscar wasn't an infrequent sight around the house through these early days of summer, but this was the first time she felt she had the right to touch him. She explored the planes of his chest, fingertips dipping into the valleys, climbing the peaks, trailing along the curves of his shoulders. All while he was unfastening his jeans with one hand. She traced a path south, surveying the newly bared flesh, and when he shoved his pants down his thighs, his rigid cock bounced up, slapping his stomach. Thick and long, the cut head mushroomed out, a trail of liquid shining along the flesh.

Lindy wrapped her hand around and gave an experimental slide, rewarded when Oscar's head tipped back again with a grunted, "*Fuck*," as he thrust into her hand.

Drunk on his response, she wanted more and didn't give him any warning, just folded to her knees and took the head of his cock into her mouth, teasing with the flat of her tongue, alternating that with hard sucks. She kept her hand sliding slowly up and down and angled her head so she could look up Oscar's body into his face. He'd dipped his chin to his throat, his expression darkening, lips curling into a silent snarl as he watched her work him. He cupped her cheek, fingers trailing to trace her lips where they caressed him. Then he wrapped a hand around the base of his cock and angled it towards her mouth.

With his obvious pleasure in what she was doing, she continued to lick and suck, lapping at the tip like a lollipop before taking him deeper. They kept on like that until Lindy was eager to see how far she could take him, wanting to make him feel good. His hips were moving, controlled thrusts that had enough slap and force at the end to push him farther into her mouth with every stroke, even as he took care not to gag her. "Lindy." Her name was a dark rumble, and she went at him harder, wanting with everything in her to hear that again, and again. "Lindy, fuck, baby."

She'd just bent her head to the task again when he pulled out of her mouth, curled over her, and lifted. In moments he'd divested her of shirt and bra, and any annoyance she felt at losing the chance to have her mouth on him disappeared the moment her breasts were freed as he dove close, laving her nipple gently. With an inrush of breath at the sensation of his lips, tongue, and beard against her skin, she cradled his head to her as he worked her breast with his mouth, fingers busy at the waist of her pants. Jeans and undies on the floor, he picked her up and took the two steps to his bed, placing her in the center with a gentle toss.

Separated from his touch and heat, she lifted her head, remembering her exasperation at being interrupted. "Oscar, I was enjoying myself."

"Oh, yeah. You were about thirty seconds from that bein' the only enjoyment you got out of the deal, other than my fingers and my mouth. Woman, you can suck my cock as much as you want any other time, swear to God. Swear to God." He stroked her face, a caress of her cheek that ended with his thumb rolling across her lips. "Just not this time." He stretched out beside her, his thigh across her hips meaning she felt the pressure of his erection closer to where she wanted it. She rocked up, reveling in the heat and pressure, and he rumbled her name again, "Lindy," a warning and acknowledgment in one.

Then his mouth was on hers, tongues dueling, and she lost herself in his kiss, as she always did. They were a drug she'd come to crave, the taste of him better than any fine wine she'd ever had. She curled her hand around his wrist and tugged, bringing it from where he gripped her waist to her breast, and he immediately set to doing what she wanted. Fingers caressing, fingertips and nails scratching, tugging lightly at her nipple until it tingled and drew pulses of pleasure from between her legs. His mouth left hers, traveling along her neck, over her chest, positioning so his tongue lapped again at her nipple, fingers feeding her into his mouth where he drew gently, alternating sucks with nips from his teeth, while his fingers found their way to the center of her.

She spread her legs, and he covered her pussy with his palm, rocking against her clit while a fingertip circled her entrance.

On an inrush of breath, she begged, "Please, honey."

He moved, mouth following the route his hand had taken, and a moment later, the hot, wet pressure of his tongue was on her and Lindy arched up against the feeling, already soaring. Eyes closed, she sank into the sensation of his tongue and teeth, the grip of a firm bite on the inside of her thigh, the roughened scrape of his beard. His name drifted from her on an exhale when he tormented with his fingers and then gave up the teasing, sinking first one, then two fingers inside her, his mouth staying latched to her clit. She tensed, back arching up as the soaring became a rocket's arc, heading to the stratosphere with an explosion before drifting back down, slowly. Oscar gave her time to recover, showing he didn't mind doing it, his mouth and hands moving on her in ways that made her heart race even as her body slid into a sluggish languor.

"Lindy, you ready for me?" She hummed at his question, blinking up at him in time to see his smile appear from behind the corner of a sheet, beard slicked down from the swipe he'd taken at it. She still had his hand between her legs, fingers sliding in the slippery evidence of everything he'd just given her. He'd rocked back on his heels, knees spread wide, and his cock jutted out from his body at an upward angle. She took in the sight of him for a moment—broad chest dusted with dark hair, hand balled into a fist on his thick thigh, other arm moving slowly in time with the touches he was giving her.

When she nodded, he smiled wider, teeth shining through his beard as she told him, "So ready."

He reached past her, leaning over on a stiffened arm. She felt the promise of heat all along her body from his closeness. The nightstand rattled, and she watched, enthralled, as he covered himself in a condom, his shaking fingers exposing how much this meant to him. Then she had more than the promise of heat, because he was blazing, and his skin was like silk against hers, his weight exactly what she hadn't known she craved.

Cocking her knees up, she gripped his hips with her thighs and arched her back. Gaze locked to his, she whispered, "Please, Oscar. I need you."

***

Oscar

Her words lit a fire inside him, the flames consuming any doubts and fears in an instant, and he leaned in to press his mouth to hers. He kissed her gently, soaking in the sensation, and when she whimpered into his mouth, he slid inside her on a slow glide, pushing steadily until he was rooted, deep as he could go.

"God, baby." He broke the kiss to take a breath, trying to tamp down the demand of his body to move fast and hard, wanting this first time to be something they both held to going forwards. Something to remember and build from. Together. *Me and her.* His balls had already drawn up tight, the coiled need in his belly growing hard to ignore. "So perfect, so absolutely fuckin' perfect." He shoved up on an elbow and raked a hand up her hip and side, fingers closing around the soft globe of her breast. "You fit everything about me." He rolled her nipple and tugged, then groaned when that earned her pussy tightening around him, clamping down in a milking ripple of pressure. "Everything about you is what I need."

"Oscar," she whispered, eyes half-mast and dark, pupils wide with everything she was feeling. Everything he was giving her. Her hips lifted, and he felt her heels against his ass, pressing him into her. "Please, baby. Move."

"Anything you need, Lindy." He pulled out an inch, then plunged back inside her, the thud as he hit her pubic bone resonating through his dick. "Anything." Another slow retreat, farther, then the same hard thrust to get back to where he belonged. "Anything for you." Her pussy grasped at him when he slid out again, and she whined far back in her throat, her body drawn tight and tense with anticipation. He dipped in, back out, then in again, over and over, moving slowly and gently, until he pounded into her hard, regaining all his lost ground in a rush. Unable to breathe for the beauty of Lindy lost to passion, Oscar bent his head to the notch of her shoulder, lips to her skin.

That was the pace he tried to hold to for as long as his body allowed, and they quickly fell into a natural rhythm. She lifted her head and worked at his throat with her mouth, nails dragging along his ribs in a trail of pain that was exactly what he needed. Her muffled cries were as demanding as her pussy, legs wrapped tight around him, feet beating a bouncing tattoo against his ass with every thrust. She tightened and called out, hips rocking up faster, and he grunted at the demand of her hot and tight pussy pulling him deeper. Oscar thrust a hand between them, arrowed his thumb to her clit, and rolled, strummed, and pressed until she stiffened with another cry, this his name. Her climax worked to pull him over the edge, a leap he was happy to take with her, freefalling through time and space inside her and over her, protecting her and giving her everything. His words came out jumbled, but he meant everything he told her as he thrust deep, then deeper, then held while his cock jerked, filling the condom with heat.

"Anything. Gonna give you everything. You and Chris. Mine. My world, baby. My whole world."

Chapter Eight
Oscar

Handle of the stroller gripped tight in one hand, he bent his neck as he called her name, "Lindy," so when she looked up questioningly, he could take her mouth. He loved doing that, surprising her with affection, especially out in the open where everyone could see. She'd told him one night that looking back at her time spent with the jackhole, he hadn't wanted any public displays, which in retrospect she understood was a telltale. Oscar liked moving them along the path of being together in a way that there was no comparison between the before and the now.

When he regretfully ended the kiss, they'd stopped stock-still on the sidewalk, and the expression on her face was everything he wanted, soft and warm, loving and sweet, and oh-so-slightly dazed. He jostled her with the arm wrapped around her shoulder, prompting her with a gentle, "Say yes."

She blinked and frowned, then the corner of her mouth tipped up in that damned crooked grin that always, always took his breath away. Lifting one eyebrow, she told him, "Yes?"

He nodded and quickly dropped his gaze to Chris, who he wagered would be patient for about thirty more seconds before he started yelling and rocking back and forth in his impatient efforts to get the stroller moving again. Their boy knew they were headed to the playground, and he loved the tiny jungle gym there. Oscar dropped his arm and grabbed her right hand, placed it on the stroller's handle, then dug in his pocket. Wrapping his hand around her left one, he raised it to his lips and softly kissed the backs of her knuckles as he slipped the ring into place. "You're gonna marry me."

Lindy gasped and stared at him, but the pleasure in her surprise was exactly what he'd been hoping to see.

"Aren't you supposed to do that the other way around? And isn't it intended to be a question?"

"Have you met me?" He scoffed, then leaned in to kiss her softly, holding her fingers to his chest, right over his thundering heart. If she felt his nervousness, she didn't show it, kissing him back then smiling against his lips when Chris yodeled his displeasure down the street, the stroller making a racket as he wiggled around. "When do I follow the normal path on anything? I met you when you were havin' my baby." He didn't miss the softening

of her expression, something that happened every time
he called Chris his, and he couldn't wait until he stopped
getting that, which would mean she understood it was
just how he felt. "Moved you into my house before we
had a single date"—she rolled her eyes—"and told you
just how I much I loved you before we slept together."
She tipped her head to the side, and he shrugged, kissing
her again. "Okay, maybe that last one was the right
order, but you gotta admit, I'm all about the thrill of
you."

"The thrill of me?"

"Oh, yeah, baby. Every day with you?" Chris yodeled
again, voice rising to a squawk at the end, and Oscar saw
the stroller jitter forwards and back a few inches. He
turned and wrapped his arm around Lindy again, taking
up the happy duty of pushing his son towards a place
where he could play safely and Oscar could feel up the
boy's momma happily. "Every day's a thrill."

~~~

THANK YOU

Thank you so much for reading *Pucker Factor*, book three in my Mayhan Bucklers MC series. These stories have a dear place in my heart, and I hope you've enjoyed them all.

ABOUT THE AUTHOR

Raised in the south, MariaLisa learned about the magic of books at an early age. Every summer, she would spend hours in the local library, devouring books of every genre. Self-described as a book-a-holic, she says "I've always loved to read, but then I discovered writing, and found I adored that, too. For reading...if nothing else is available, I've been known to read the back of the cereal box."

Also by MariaLisa deMora

Alace Sweets

A dark thriller, this book is not a light read. Filled with edge-of-your-seat suspense, this intense story commands the reader's attention as it drives towards the explosive ending. Alace Sweets is a vigilante serial killer, with everything that implies and is sure to trip all your triggers. Be ready.

At seventeen, Alace Sweets turned a corner in her life, taking the wrong shortcut home from school.

Resisting the harsh knowledge her attackers will never be made to pay for their actions, Alace takes a stand. Justice must be served, and if fate's scales are out of balance, she's determined to set things right as best she can.

When the laws of men fail, the rules of Alace prevail.

5-Star Reviews for Alace Sweets

"deMora has a superb story-line and exceptional character development. All of her characters have such depth that will intrigue the reader..."
~Turning Another Page

"Hot, sweet, dark thriller."
~Beth D

"It will keep you on the edge of your seat and give you chills."
~Escape Reality Book Blog

"Disturbing, haunting, sickly; yet hot, sexy and heart racing!"
~Amanda L

"From the first page [deMora] pulls you into the world she has created and you do not even try to escape..."
~Little Shop of Readers Blog

"A must read for all those dark, gritty romance fans out there."
~Sweet & Spicy Reads

"You will find yourself so drawn into the story that the outside world is blocked out and your locking the doors and turning on all the lights."
~Danena F

"Don't judge me for bonding with a vigilante serial killer, she's more than what she does."
~iScream Books

"Thrilling...chilling...full of suspense, nail biting edge of your seat excitement."
~Tracey H

"Every time MariaLisa deMora picks up her pen (or opens her computer), she creates characters you want to believe in."
~Gail S

"Intriguing dark storyline, beautiful love story and nail-biting conclusion, what more could a reader ask for?"
~Manda M

"This book takes you a dark and twisted ride that is gripping..."
~Renee Entress' Blog

"This book is dark and gritty and I literally had to take a day off from reading it because it's that intense."
~My Girlfriend's Couch

"This is my favourite book so far from this author ... I recommend this book if you enjoy dark romantic thrillers."
~Cheekypee Reads and Reviews

"There's not enough stars to give this book and 5 just doesn't really do it justice!"
~DeLane C

"I couldn't put this book down from page one! Tried to stop & go to bed but couldn't sleep thinking about Alace and got up & finished the book."
~Debbie M

"MariaLisa DeMora, wordsmith that she is, made this a story of the enlightenment of a woman and finding love in a life where she has had none."
~Kat W

"Whatever deep dark trench [deMora] pulled a character like Alace from should be revisited again and often."
~Confessions of a Serial Reader

ADDITIONAL SERIES AND BOOKS

Please note that books in a series frequently feature characters from additional books within that series. If series books are read out of order, readers will twig to spoilers for the other books, so going back to read the skipped titles won't have the same angsty reveals.

Rebel Wayfarers MC series:

Mica, #1
A Sweet & Merry Christmas, #1.5
Slate, #2
Bear, #3
Jase, #4
Gunny, #5
Mason, #6
Hoss, #7
Harddrive Holidays, #7.5
Duck, #8
Biker Chick Campout, #8.5
Watcher, #9
A Kiss to Keep You, #9.25
Gun Totin' Annie, #9.5
Secret Santa, #9.75
Bones, #10
Gunny's Pups, #10.25
Never Settle, #10.5
Not Even A Mouse, #10.75
Fury, #11
Christmas Doings, #11.25
Gypsy's Lady, #11.5
Cassie, #12
Road Runner's Ride, #12.5

Occupy Yourself band series:

Born Into Trouble, #1
Grace In Motion, #2 (TBD)
What They Say, #3 (TBD)

Neither This, Nor That MC series:

This Is the Route Of Twisted Pain, #1
Treading the Traitor's Path: Out Bad, #2
Shelter My Heart, #3
Trapped by Fate on Reckless Roads, #4
Thunderstruck, #5

Mayhan Bucklers MC series:

Most Rikki-Tik, #1
Mad Minute, #2
Pucker Factor, #3

If You Could Change One Thing: Tangled Fates Stories

There Are Limits, #1
Rules Are Rules, #2
The Gray Zone, #3

Other Books:

With My Whole Heart
Alace Sweets
Hard Focus

More information available at mldemora.com.